Faces in the Dust

Pinkerton Detective Ward Loman rode into Coldwater, Texas to hunt down the killer Leo Slattery. His orders were to take Leo in dead or alive. But there was trouble on the local range involving Leo's family, headed by Hub Slattery, owner of the HS ranch.

As the situation rapidly worsens, Loman comes to the rescue of Kate Hesp, and is plunged into a deadly sequence of events with its origins in the war between North and South. A gold shipment had disappeared in the last weeks of the war and this was a mystery that would not go away.

Just as Loman expected, gunsmoke and death would be the outcome.

By the same author

Range Grab
Bank Raid
Range Wolves
Gun Talk
Violent Trail
Lone Hand
Gunsmoke Justice
Big Trouble
Gun Peril
War at the Diamond O
Twisted Trail
Showdown at Singing Springs
Blood and Grass
The Hanna Gang
Raven's Feud
Hell Town

Faces in the Dust

CORBA SUNMAN

ROBERT HALE · LONDON

First published in Great Britain 2005

ISBN 0 7090 7837 4

Robert Hale Limited
Clerkenwell House
Clerkenwell Green
London EC1R 0HT

Typeset by
Derek Doyle & Associates, Shaw Heath.
Printed and bound in Great Britain by
Antony Rowe Limited, Wiltshire

ONE

Ward Loman was a long time reaching Coldwater; far longer than he had estimated because the desert country of south-west Texas, with its rarefied air, had that effect on distance and objects. A horse and rider could be seen miles away, and the mountains to the west never seemed to draw closer, no matter how long a man travelled in their direction. He was experienced in travelling the back trails and lonely places, for his job as a Pinkerton Agency detective depended upon anonymity. His name was famed for fighting criminals, but his face was practically unknown, and his survival depended on his ability to keep it that way. Every crooked hand was against him; hence his practice of riding into a town after the sun had set.

He urged his dun horse along a little faster, a tall, lean man in his early thirties, with a hawklike face and cold blue eyes, whose instincts had been honed and sharpened by the vagaries of his way of life. He had the intent gaze of a predatory rattlesnake, missing nothing of his surroundings, and always ready to strike if his reflexes gave warning of danger. As he rode he glanced frequently over his shoulder, satisfying himself that his back trail was empty, and always checked ahead that no hidden gun was waiting for him to get within range. He was keenly aware that his life depended upon his caution and skill with a gun. He had flirted with the tough, lawless element of the West in order to fight and vanquish them.

He reached the outskirts of Coldwater as the sun disappeared behind the distant mountains. Usually he was interested only in obtaining supplies and leaving without attracting attention to himself, but Coldwater, in Tate County, was different. Leo Slattery had once lived here, and word was that he was heading back this way to visit with his family. Loman wanted Leo for murder, but he was in no hurry, aware that in this country a man making haste could only highlight himself.

He reined in and studied the main street, with its dilapidated adobe buildings. Music and noise were coming from at least three saloons, and there were lights in the tall windows of a grain store, where a late customer was loading sacks into a wagon.

He rode along the centre of the street, where beams of lamplight reflecting from the buildings on either side just failed to meet, leaving a narrow avenue of shadow. He had to take care of his horse. The animal had covered too many miles on the trail without a decent rest since he had quit New Mexico after smashing the Yaro gang. If he needed to leave in a hurry he would soon be afoot. He realized that he would have to spend a few days in Coldwater – the horse needed rest even if he didn't.

There was a livery barn at the end of the street, and he stabled the animal and took care of its needs before going to the office in a corner, where a youth was seated at a table, looking through a child's picture book, his lips moving slowly as he tried to read the simple legends under the illustrations.

Loman flipped a silver dollar on to the dusty surface of the table, startling the youngster, who looked up quickly.

'The dun horse in the first stall,' Loman said. 'It'll be here a couple of days. Give it a drink in about half an hour, and then grain it. I'll be along later to look it over.'

The youth nodded, picked up the dollar, and returned his attention to the book. Loman turned away and lost himself in the shadows when he left the barn. He needed to feed and water himself, but wanted to get to the general store before it closed for the night. He had finished the last of his supplies that morning, and had no wish to quit town with an empty gunny sack. He had learned some hard lessons in the time he had been a Pinkerton man, and never underestimated the bad men against whom he waged ceaseless war.

He was about to enter a restaurant when he heard a woman cry out somewhere close by. The shadows were dense and he halted, his right hand dropping to the butt of his pistol. Placing his back against a wall, he looked around with narrowed eyes, using his ears as well as his sight. The silence was heavy, although he could hear the muted sound of music coming from one of the saloons further along the street. He strained his ears, wondering if he had imagined the cry. It had sounded like a woman was in trouble – perhaps in pain.

Tense moments passed while he waited and listened. Then he told himself that it was none of his business and turned to the door of the eating-house, aware that whatever was going on, he could not afford to get involved. As he grasped the handle of the door the cry was repeated, and this time it was laced with pain, and rising into a thin scream that sounded like pure terror.

Loman thought the cries had come from the building opposite, which was in darkness, and were of such intensity he could not ignore them. He went across the street with long strides, right hand hovering over the butt of his pistol, his left hand clenched into a big fist. He saw movement in an alley next to the building and, as he stepped on to the sidewalk, a large figure emerged from the alley to confront him.

'Where do you think you're going?' a harsh voice challenged.

'I heard a woman scream,' Loman replied.

'Someone is teaching his wife a lesson. You better get on outa here. It ain't none of your business.'

'Help me,' a woman called from the darkness of the alley, her voice betraying stark terror. 'Please help me.'

Loman heard the scrape of metal against leather and reached out quickly with his left hand. He caught hold of a wrist as the big stranger drew a pistol from his holster, and held it motionless as he sledged his right fist against a bristled chin, his whole body-weight behind the punch. The man uttered a groan and slumped to the ground. Loman kicked away the pistol that thudded on the sidewalk.

An orange gun-flash tore through the black void in the alley, spurting towards Loman, and it illuminated the figures of a man and a woman. The woman was being held by the man. Loman saw her pale face clearly before the flash died, and he heard a .45 slug crackle past the lobe of his right ear as he pressed against the side of the alley before lunging forward to make contact with the pair. He hit the man solidly with his right shoulder, a hand sweeping out to snatch the uplifted pistol, and the weapon exploded again, hurling raucous echoes through the darkness and almost deafening Loman. The flash dazzled Loman's eyes, but he landed a punch on the man's chin and heard the pistol thud on the ground.

The fingers of his left hand found the woman's arm and he held her as rapidly departing footsteps indicated the man's flight along the alley to the back lots. He felt her pull away, but held on, talking soothingly.

'I won't hurt you,' he rasped. 'I was passing and heard your cries. How many men were bothering you?'

'Let's get away from here quickly,' she replied tensely. 'The sheriff will come running because of the shots.'

Loman pulled her out of the alley, and was in time to catch a glimpse of the big man he had knocked down making off fast along the sidewalk to disappear into another alley. Gun echoes were reverberating across the town, and Loman sighed, for the last thing he had wanted was attention drawn to himself.

'What was going on?' he asked, trying to get a look at her face, but there was not enough light to reveal details. 'Who were those men? Why did you scream?'

'I think they were after money.' Her voice was now well-controlled. 'Thank you for coming to my aid. I'm all right now. I'd better go before the sheriff shows up. I don't want him to know I was disobeying him. He's always talking about the dangers of a woman being out alone.'

'Where do you live? The least I can do is see you home safely. Those men might be hanging around until I leave in order to make another attempt on you.'

'I live on a ranch out of town. I have a couple of cowhands to pick up before I go home. I shall be all right now. Thank you again.'

'What ranch?' Loman grasped her arm as she turned to slip away.

'Please let me go! I can hear someone coming, and it will surely be the sheriff. I don't want to be here half the night answering his questions. I'm obliged to you, and if there's any way I can repay your help then come out to Double H and ask for me – Kate Hesp.'

She jerked her arm out of Loman's grasp and darted across the street to vanish into the shadows. Loman could hear heavy footsteps approaching along the sidewalk and turned to hurry to the restaurant. He heard a shout from along the street but ignored it. He entered the restaurant and sat down at a corner table. A waitress approached for his order and he gave it with half his attention on the street door. As the waitress departed, the door was opened and a tall figure entered to pause and look over the dozen or so diners.

Loman turned his face from the newcomer, filled with sudden consternation, for he recognized the tall, broad-shouldered man as one of the many who rode the back trails making a living from his skill with a gun. He searched his mind for a name and came up with James Sorgan. They had worked together once, shooting rustlers for Lou Davidson's Big D ranch in Arizona. That had been nine years ago, and now Sorgan was here, wearing a sheriff's law star, his dark features expressing determination mingled with a great deal of pressure.

The waitress approached to set a cup of coffee before Loman. Sorgan called to her and she crossed to him. Loman drank coffee, keeping his face averted from Sorgan, and was relieved when the sheriff departed. The waitress came back to Loman's table.

'Your meal will be ready in a moment,' she said pleasantly. 'The sheriff said to tell you he'd like to see you in his office when you've eaten.'

Loman nodded and raised the coffee cup to his lips. The waitress retreated into the kitchen. Loman sighed heavily. Sorgan had seen and recognized him. His anonymity was broken, but he would have to contact the local law before commencing operations in this county, and it was better that he knew Sorgan instead of coming up against a stranger who might turn awkward.

The waitress returned shortly with his order and he ate hungrily, his mind working on the situation. He would have to see Sorgan, but did not expect trouble from the lawman. Sorgan knew nothing of Loman's connection with Pinkerton, and the fact that Sorgan was now wearing a law badge could prove to be an advantage.

His meal finished, Loman went out to the street, where he paused, thinking of Kate Hesp. What kind of trouble was she in? He was certain the two men who had accosted her were not ordinary hold-up men and if there was local trouble then he knew better than to become involved, even if a woman was implicated. He walked along the sidewalk to the law office. He had to stick around the county to check on Leo Slattery, so he had better make contact with the local law.

A tall figure stood in the open doorway of the law office, watching the street, and Loman went forward grimly. James Sorgan half-turned into the office and lamplight spilled over his fleshy face. He was big and well-muscled, dressed in a blue store-suit that was a shade too tight at the shoulders. The brim of a flat-crowned grey plains hat was pulled low over brown eyes that gleamed as they regarded Loman's set features. His jacket was unbuttoned, and Loman saw an ornate gun belt around Sorgan's waist that he remembered so well.

A smile touched Sorgan's fleshy lips and he extended his right hand, his manner friendly.

'Good to see you again, Ward. What's brought you

to Coldwater? The last I heard, you were in New Mexico.'

Loman shook hands. 'I'm hunting a killer,' he said. 'His family lives around here.' He studied the law star on Sorgan's shirt front. 'How you doing, James? I've wondered some about you since we worked together for Lou Davidson.'

'This is just another job.' Sorgan lifted his hand to touch the law badge with his thumb. 'They made me an offer I couldn't refuse. Come on in and let's talk.'

Sorgan moved into the office, stepping aside for Loman to enter, and closed the door when he had done so.

'Were you involved in that shooting I heard some time ago?' he asked.

'Yeah.' Loman described the incident and saw Sorgan's expression change. He was harassed, Loman could see, which was unusual for a man of the sheriff's calibre, and Loman was intrigued.

'Who was the woman?' Sorgan demanded.

Loman shook his head. 'It was dark. I didn't get a look at her face, and she hurried off like I was poison.'

'How was she dressed?'

'That I can't tell you either. It was too dark to see.'

'What about the two men? Did you get a look at them?'

'Nope. They were in an alley where the light didn't reach. I might be able to recognize the voice of one of them, but that's the best I could do.'

'You said you're on the trail of a killer who has family around here. What's his name?'

'Leo Slattery. He left home a long time ago. I heard he was heading back here so I need to check him out.'

Sorgan nodded. 'I think Leo's family are mixed up in the trouble I'm having here. I haven't seen Leo around. He was against us in Arizona, if I remember rightly, Ward. I've got plenty of trouble coming up. If you catch up with Leo, take him out of my bailiwick before you shoot him.' He paused as if a sudden idea had struck him. 'Maybe you can help me out while you're waiting for him to show up.'

'Sure, if I can.'

'I'm planning on getting hitched later this year, and I could do with someone like you riding herd on my gal and keeping trouble from hitting her folks.'

'Congratulations. What's her name?'

'Kate Hesp. Her father owns the Double H ranch north of here. There's a range war simmering between Hesp and his neighbour, Hub Slattery, who has two other hell-raising sons besides Leo – Charlie and Wes. I've made Slattery pull in his horns some, and taught both his sons to respect the law, but life is uneasy, and I got the feeling that all hell will bust loose when I least expect it. It's like sitting on a powder-keg with a fuse burning.'

Loman digested the information without changing his expression. No wonder Kate had wanted to get away before Sorgan showed up. She was engaged to him. He wondered at the implications that had taken her into the alley with the two unknown men. He nodded, despite a desire not to become involved in local troubles. His natural curiosity was aroused, and it could do no harm to visit Double H and learn more of the situation. He had already learned that Leo Slattery's family were neighbours of the Hesps – that Leo was not around yet – and wondered at the complications that might arise from the situation.

'I'll help if I can, James,' he decided. 'I had planned to get supplies and be on my way before morning, but if Leo hasn't showed up yet then I'll have to stick around to see if he does.'

'That's good, Ward. Hang around for a spell. I can make you a deputy. A law badge would sure as hell give you a lot of weight. Think about it, will you?'

'Sure, and thanks for the offer. It might be just what I need right now. I'll talk to you some more tomorrow, huh? Right now I need to stock up on supplies. I never know when I might have to split the breeze. Would you want I should take a riding job at Double H to keep an eye on Kate?'

'I'd appreciate it if you'd nose around some. See if you can find out what's doing behind the scenes. Someone is pushing for trouble, and it ain't necessarily the Slattery boys. I suspect this is one of those deep-game jobs. Some crooked operator is covering his tracks by pointing the blame against others.'

'It'd be a change to work with the law,' Loman bluffed with a grin.

Sorgan went to the desk and took a deputy badge from a drawer. He flipped it into Loman's ready hand and Loman pinned it to his shirt-front.

'Raise your right hand and I'll swear you in,' Sorgan said.

Loman did so, and repeated the solemn statement

that Sorgan uttered.

'That's all there is to it,' Sorgan told him. 'You're free to go around the county as you please. I know you'll uphold the law if you see it being broken.'

'Thanks. I'll bring my chores up to date, and then take a look around your town. I'll ride out to Double H tomorrow.'

'You shouldn't find any trouble. The place is quiet at the moment, but don't take my word for it. Hell is likely to bust out any time. I can smell trouble around here, but I can't put a finger on it or bring it out into the open.'

Loman went out to the street, thinking over the situation. Kate Hesp had certainly been in a lot of trouble when she called for help. He decided that he would like to have a talk with the two men responsible for the girl's problems, and headed for the nearest saloon. He had not seen faces in the alley, but had noted the voice of the big stranger who had first accosted him, and thought he might recognize it again if he heard it.

He blinked at the glare of the lamps in the saloon when he pushed through the batwings, and stood for a few moments to enable his eyes to adjust. There were more than a score of men inside, and the few small tables to the left were occupied by intent gamblers. Eight men were bellied up to the bar, drinking, and they all glanced towards the doorway at Loman's entrance. He walked to the near corner of the bar, conscious of the silver star pinned to his shirt-front. Perhaps it was not such a good idea to set up as an open target. He had always preferred to remain in the background. His work as a detective in these troubled times was hectic, and death was always at his shoulder.

A tender came towards him, cloth in hand, wiping the bar top instinctively. His narrowed brown eyes went to the badge on Loman's shirt and his expression hardened as he took in Loman's appearance.

'You're new in town.' The tender was an old man with small, dark eyes and lank hair hanging over his greasy forehead. He was running to seed, overweight, with a manner that suggested he had learned all the tricks of his trade. 'I'm Jake Dabner. Sorgan was saying he needed another deputy. Al Donovan, the other deputy, ain't much use, and I reckon he would run at the first shot. What can I get you? Your first drink is on the house.'

'Beer.' Loman looked around more closely, taking in the faces of his drinking companions. The level of conversation had fallen at his entrance and all eyes were upon him, but gazes fell away when he met them, and then activity was resumed.

The barkeep looked like he wanted to say more, but Loman's taciturn manner dissuaded him. He went back along the bar, poured a beer, and sent the foaming glass sliding along the bar top to stop directly in front of Loman. Thirst was racking Loman's throat and he half-emptied the glass with long gulps before leaning an elbow on the bar.

A man entered the saloon and walked along the bar to someone standing alone at the far end. Loman watched the newcomer's progress, and his keen gaze spotted that the man was wearing a gun belt with an empty holster. He straightened and centred his attention on the two men, who put their heads together and talked quietly. The newcomer was tall and slim, a young man of around thirty, dressed in range clothes and having all the earmarks of a ranch hand. The second man was older and bigger, well fleshed out, with narrowed blue eyes that seemed to be constantly weighing up his chances. He was wearing a store suit with a gun belt buckled around his waist under the jacket, and it was some moments before Loman saw that the holster was empty.

Loman drained his glass and set it down loudly on the bar. Dabner looked in his direction and Loman pushed his glass forward a few inches. Dabner came along the bar.

'Another?' he enquired.

'Yeah. Who is the guy that just came in?'

Dabner glanced along the bar. 'Clem Bellamy – rides for HS, Hub Slattery's brand. The man he's talking to is Joseph Aird, a local cattle-buyer. Do you want a rundown on everyone in the place?'

'Not right now. And forget the beer.'

Loman stepped away from the bar, and was about to walk towards Bellamy and Aird when he heard the batwings creak. He jerked his head around to check. Two cowhands were entering the saloon and paused on the threshold, looking around intently. Loman, able to smell trouble a mile away, recognized instantly that they were on the prod. He straightened.

'He's down at the far end,' one of the cowboys said, and the other nodded.

'Let's go get him,' he responded.

They came forward together, hands resting on the butts of their holstered guns. Loman pushed himself away from the bar to step in front of them, primed to handle his first job as a deputy.

TWO

The cowboys paused when Loman confronted them. They looked him up and down, and their intent expressions changed when they spotted the deputy badge on his shirt front.

'You got something on your mind, gents?' Loman asked.

'Who in hell are you?' demanded the taller of the two. His tone was aggressive: anger mingled with determination.

'I'm gonna shoot holes in that pair at the end of the bar,' the smaller, thickset man said hotly. 'I ain't gonna stand by while the likes of them insult the boss's daughter.'

'You talking about Bellamy and Aird?' Loman demanded.

'Who else? And don't try to stop us, Deputy. You're a stranger, and might not know that Kate Hesp and the sheriff are getting hitched later this year.'

'I know about it, so why don't you tell the sheriff what's on your mind and let him handle what is his business?'

'We ride for Double H, and a thing like this is up to us. We came into town with Miss Kate, and we're supposed to keep an eye open for her.'

'So where were you while she was walking the town alone after nightfall?'

'How do you know she was out alone?'

'I happened to be on hand to stop the two men who accosted her, and I've just worked out that they are the two at the end of the bar. How do *you* know they are the men?'

'Miss Kate told us.'

'So she knew them, and wouldn't tell me.' Loman smiled. 'You better get back to her pronto. Something bad could be happening to her right now, and you still ain't watching her like you should be. Leave those two at the end of the bar to me. I was about to arrest them when you walked in.'

'Go ahead and do it.'

Loman smiled. 'I got you pegged right,' he said, 'so let us get acquainted before we go any further. Just who am I talking to?'

'Curly Jackson,' said the tall, thin cowhand. He was about thirty. His pale eyes twinkled, and a sheepish smile touched his lips as he met Loman's gaze.

'I'm Fred Emmet.' The other was older, in his mid-thirties, and hard-bitten. Emotion was showing in his dark eyes, and his lips had a malicious twist. 'You ain't just gonna arrest those two, are you? They need to be taught a lesson for what they did. We should take them along to the stable and whale the tar outa them.'

'They'll get what's coming to them,' Loman

responded. 'Now get out of here and I'll do my job.'

They turned reluctantly and departed. Loman waited until the batwings had finished swinging behind them before turning to face the end of the bar. He realized that the whole saloon had overhead what passed between him and the two Double H riders, and Bellamy and Aird were not waiting to be braced. Both men were making for the side door.

'Hold it right there,' Loman called. 'I need to talk to you.'

Bellamy kept walking, but Aird turned instantly, his right hand lifting to slide under his jacket towards the left armpit.

'I told you to hold it,' Loman repeated, flexing the fingers of his gun hand.

Aird continued his movement, and Loman waited until he saw the glint of lamplight on metal as Aird brought a small-calibre pistol into action before setting his hand into motion. His .45 cleared leather and exploded deafeningly before Aird could shoot, and his slug hit the cattle buyer in the right shoulder. Bellamy halted and raised his hands as Aird pitched forward on to his face on the sawdusted boards. Loman, his face impassive, stood motionless, pistol ready, a dribble of gun smoke curling from its muzzle.

Loman went forward and kicked aside the gun Aird had dropped. He grasped Bellamy's right shoulder and pulled the man around to face him. Bellamy's features were ashen, his eyes filled with shock.

'Why the trouble?' Loman demanded. 'You and

Aird must be feeling mighty guilty about something to resist the law.'

'We heard what Jackson and Emmet told you. They were looking for an excuse to start shooting at us. Maybe you don't know about it, but there's trouble between HS and Double H.'

'Where's your pistol?' Loman asked, and saw Bellamy's expression change.

'I don't carry it in town in case any Double H rider is looking for trouble.'

'And Aird's holster is empty. Why is he wearing a gun belt if he relies on a shoulder holster?'

'You better ask him.'

'I shall, when he's able to talk.' Loman nodded. 'Two men attacked Kate Hesp in an alley some minutes ago. I disarmed both of them before they ran away. I suspect you and Aird were those two men, so I'm taking you in for questioning.'

'You've got the wrong men,' Bellamy replied.

Loman shook his head. 'Kate Hesp named you and Aird. That's why Jackson and Emmet showed up here looking for you.' He paused when the batwings creaked open, and threw a glance in that direction. Sorgan was entering, pistol in hand. The sheriff paused and looked around, then came forward grimly.

Loman explained what had happened and Sorgan nodded his approval. He bent over the groaning Aird and examined the man's wound.

'He'll live,' he said callously. 'Bellamy, I've warned you more than once to pull in your horns. So what were you and Aird doing together, and attacking Kate?'

'We were only talking to her,' Bellamy said tightly.

'In a dark alley?' Loman rapped. 'I heard a woman scream, and when I came to the alley you fired a shot at me without attempting to find out who I was.'

'Let's get along to the office.' Sorgan turned and looked at the intent faces watching them with close interest. 'Brewer, go fetch the doc to Aird, and stay with him until I come for him.'

A man left the saloon hurriedly, and Sorgan addressed another spectator.

'Jake, watch Aird until the doc arrives.'

The man in question nodded, and Sorgan motioned to Bellamy.

'You know where the jail is so head for it. I'll want some straight answers from you, so set your mind to telling the truth.'

Bellamy walked to the batwings and Loman followed closely. They left the saloon and Bellamy led the way along the sidewalk to the law office. Sorgan caught up with them as they entered. Bellamy sat down on a chair beside the desk. He looked apprehensive, but seemed resigned to the situation. Sorgan sat down behind the desk, and for a moment he regarded Bellamy silently, then leaned back in his seat and folded his arms.

'Tell it like it happened, Bellamy,' he said quietly. 'I want to know everything, and don't forget that the woman we're talking about is my future wife. I'll get her side of this after I've heard you out, and she'll tell me the truth, so your account better tally with hers.'

Bellamy shook his head. 'I've got nothing to say,' he responded.

Sorgan smiled and got up from his seat. 'You can have it that way if you want it,' he said mildly, and moved around the desk. 'I've been waiting patiently for someone to make a mistake in this business, and you've finally done it. Whatever happens to you now, remember that you brought it on yourself. It ain't bad enough that you attacked a female, you had to pick on my woman.'

He reached out, grasped Bellamy's shirt-front with his left hand, and hauled the man out of his seat. Bellamy protested loudly, and his voice cut off quickly when Sorgan struck him on the chin with a powerful right fist. Bellamy sagged to his knees and Sorgan hauled him upright and held him.

'This will go on until you tell me the truth,' Sorgan said tensely, and struck Bellamy again, this time allowing the man to fall to the floor.

Bellamy lay on his face, groaning, and Sorgan watched him for several moments before dragging him upright again. Bellamy was barely conscious, and raised a hand in protest.

'All right, that's enough,' he said weakly. 'I'll talk.'

'And give me the truth.' Sorgan thrust Bellamy back into the chair and held him there with a big hand. 'So how did you come to be in that alley with Aird, scaring the hell out of my future wife? I wanta know what was going on.'

'It was Aird's idea.' Bellamy fell silent, his chin touching his chest. A trickle of blood was showing at a corner of his mouth and he was breathing heavily. 'Hub Slattery sent me into town to tell Aird there was a herd of HS stock ready to be moved out. Aird had seen Kate in town and wanted her to take a message to Henry Hesp about some Double H cattle. We were on our way to the saloon for a drink when Kate came along the sidewalk.'

Bellamy lapsed into silence. Sorgan waited a few moments before cuffing him several times with an open hand. Bellamy surged up off the chair, whirling his arms ineffectually. Sorgan cuffed him again, heavily, and pushed him back into the seat.

'What are you waiting for?' Sorgan demanded. 'Get on with it. I want to know what happened. Aird wanted to pass on a business message to Henry Hesp by way of Kate, and it ended up with the two of you in an alley with her and she was calling for help. Quit stalling, Bellamy. You're up against it, and you know it. You better make this good. If I don't like your explanation I'll put you down permanent for being a no-account punk.'

'I don't know what happened. Aird spoke to Kate about Double H cattle and she told him to ride out to see her father himself because she wouldn't carry a message. She said her pa was waiting for Aird to set foot on Double H again, and the only business Aird would find was the business end of a rope. Aird lost his temper then. He grabbed Kate and shook her, and she began to call for help. Aird bundled her into the alley, and told me to hold her quiet when he heard someone coming.'

'That's when I showed up, huh?' Loman demanded.

'Yeah. You busted Aird, and I wanted to get out of there pronto. I fired a shot in the air to hold you back and ran off over the back lots. I hadn't done anything, and I was scared. It ain't good to manhandle a woman.'

'Especially my woman.' Sorgan glanced at Loman. 'Is that how you saw it, Ward?'

'When I challenged Aird he drew his pistol. I disarmed him; knocked him down. Bellamy fired at me without warning. His shot missed my right ear by about one inch. It was dark, and he was sure trying to hit me.'

Sorgan nodded. 'I'll jug him for the night and hold him until I can get the rest of the story. Put him in a cell, Ward. The keys are in the top right-hand corner of the desk. I wanta catch Kate before she rides out to Double H. Then I'll collect Aird, and we'll hear what he's got to say for himself.'

Loman nodded and took the cell keys from the drawer. Sorgan departed. Bellamy got up from the chair. He staggered as he moved towards the door in the back wall that led into the cell block, and clutched at Loman's left shoulder for support. The next instant he swung his fist at Loman's face, but missed as Loman sidestepped. Cursing, Bellamy lunged desperately at Loman, who stopped him with a left fist into his stomach. Bellamy groaned and hunched over, then fell to his knees.

'You don't learn very quickly, do you,' Loman observed. 'Get up, and come swinging if you want some more.'

Bellamy shook his head. His face was pale. He staggered to his feet and led the way into the cell block. Loman locked him in a cell and went back to the office. Sorgan returned moments later, accompanied by Kate Hesp, Curly Jackson and Fred Emmet. Sorgan introduced Loman to the girl, and they sized up each other. Loman had heard her voice but had been unable to make out any details of her in the darkness, and he was surprised by her beauty. She was tall and slender, with corn-coloured hair and keen blue eyes, and looked to be in her middle twenties. She held out her hand and Loman grasped it.

'I didn't have time to thank you properly when we met,' she said. 'And I didn't know you were acquainted with James or I wouldn't have ducked out like I did. I was hoping to avoid trouble. There's enough of that around here without me adding to it, and you came along in time to stop Aird before he went too far. No real harm was done, and I wanted to forget about it.'

'That's not how I see it,' Sorgan said sharply. 'I want to know why Aird took the step of breaking the law. Kate, what did he say to you before Ward showed up?'

'As far as I could make out he wanted me to deliver a message to my father. About cattle, I think. When I refused, he got angry, put his hands on me and shook me. That's when I cried for help, and it was fortunate that Ward appeared at that moment.'

Sorgan shook his head. 'If that was all there was to it then why did Aird try to shoot Ward? There's got to be more to it than you say, Kate. Think hard. What exactly was said before Ward showed up?'

Kate shook her head slowly. 'I've told you all I can

remember,' she said. 'I'm sure there was nothing else.'

Loman, listening intently, fancied the girl was lying and wondered what was behind her attitude. There had to be more to it than she was admitting. In the saloon Aird had reached for a gun when challenged. Loman sensed a cover-up, and wondered why Kate was protecting Bellamy and Aird.

'I'm not satisfied, Kate,' Sorgan said harshly. 'I'm convinced there is more to this than you're admitting. Why don't you come clean so I can clear up the matter? Aird has already been shot for his attitude. Why are you keeping quiet? It looks like you're shielding these men. Bellamy rides for HS, and you know there's bad blood between that outfit and your own.'

'James, you're trying too hard to solve a problem that just isn't there.' Impatience sounded in Kate's voice. 'I can only tell you what happened, and if you don't believe me then you will have to do the other thing. I'm sorry I can't be of more help, but there's nothing else I can say. Now, if you've finished with me I'll head for home.' She glanced at Loman. 'It was nice to meet you, Ward. Come out to Double H tomorrow. You'll be very welcome. You can have a chat with my father. He'll be pleased to advise you on the situation at the ranch. Perhaps you'll be able to see the truth of the situation – James certainly cannot.'

'Thanks.' Loman nodded. 'I'll ride out your way in the morning.'

'Ride out now, Ward,' Sorgan cut in. 'You'll do

more good out there than staying around town. These two cowhands can't be trusted to do their job properly or Kate wouldn't have been in that alley alone with Aird and Bellamy.'

Jackson and Emmet both began to protest but Sorgan cut them short with an uplifted hand and they fell silent, shuffling their feet in embarrassment. Kate looked as if she did not like the idea of Loman riding with her immediately, but smiled and nodded.

'I'll be happy to have your company, Ward. I'll be ready to ride in ten minutes. Be in front of the store then if you wish to accompany us.'

Loman nodded and she turned on her heel to depart hurriedly, not saying farewell to Sorgan. Jackson and Emmet hastened after the girl, then Sorgan took off his Stetson and cuffed sweat from his forehead. His face betrayed anxiety as he looked at Loman.

'What did you make of Kate's attitude, Ward?' he demanded. 'You must have seen it. Was I imagining things or is she lying about what happened?'

'I got a feeling she wasn't telling the whole truth,' Loman said diplomatically.

'So ride out to Double H with her and run your eye over the situation there. Stay a couple of days and you'll pick up the threads with no trouble. Henry Hesp is a good man, and I think he's troubled, which is not to be wondered at considering the Slattery family are his neighbours. Hub Slattery has a bad reputation around here, with his boys, Charlie and Wes, hell-raising all the time. They're running wild through the county, although I've curbed them some since I've been here. You've met Leo Slattery – a real bad 'un – and his younger brothers are not much better.'

'I'll fetch my horse and ride out,' Loman said. 'Give me a few days to look around the range before you expect me back, huh?'

'Sure thing. And don't be fooled by the way things look at the moment. It's quiet on the surface, but to my way of thinking it is too quiet, if you get what I mean.'

Loman departed, and stood for a moment on the sidewalk, thinking about Kate Hesp's attitude. He and Sorgan had been aware of her cover-up. He went along to the stable, saddled up, and was leading his horse out to the street when a dark figure showed up from the dense shadows in the rear of the big barn.

Loman palmed his pistol, and cocked the weapon.

'Hold it,' the newcomer called urgently. 'You don't need that. I'm Amos Shaw. I own this livery stable. You're a mite sudden with your gun, ain't you?'

Loman shook his head. 'Nope. Just careful,' he replied. 'What's on your mind, old-timer?'

Shaw leaned against a post. He was small, grey-haired, his dark eyes serious as he regarded Loman.

'You ain't been in town more than an hour,' he observed, 'and now you're wearing a law badge. You must know Sorgan from somewhere.'

'We rode together west of here about nine years ago.'

'You shot Joseph Aird in the saloon, I heard.'

'He made the mistake of drawing on me.'

'Well, you better watch out for him, and the men

he works with. I see a lot of what goes on at this end of the town, and generally I keep my mouth shut. I ain't one to seek trouble. But seeing that you're a lawman who's gonna hit the bad men, I reckon I can say a few words about what is happening around here. There's bad trouble acoming. I've seen and heard men talking shady business, watched money changing hands for jobs that are against the law, and got the drift of things that are due to happen in this county and, believe me, it ain't good, not by a long rope.'

'Why haven't you talked to the sheriff? He's a good lawman. He'd act on any information you could give, and he wouldn't tell who told him.'

'I'd probably wind up dead within a day of talking to him. But most folks don't know about you yet, so I can tell you a thing or two, and hope to live long enough to see you handle the situation.'

'Sure, but I don't have the time right now. I'm riding out of town for a couple of days. If you can't tell me in a few words what you've got on your mind then I'll look you up when I get back.'

'That ain't good. You need to know this right now. Henry Hesp and me – we go back a long ways. Henry set me up in this business when I couldn't ride for him any more. Busted my leg in a stampede and saved Henry from being trampled, and he appreciated it. So now he's in trouble I wanta do what I can to help him, even if I get shot for opening my mouth. Hub Slattery and his boys are stealing cattle, and some of it belongs to Double H. Aird is paying Slattery for the stolen stock, and his JA outfit is running the beeves south into Mexico. But someone else is trying to muscle in on the set-up – I heard some deep talking about that – and there'll be shooting for sure before it's settled. I can't get a line on the newcomer riding the big saddle, but he means business. That's all I can tell you, Deputy. Whatever you do, watch out for Henry Hesp, and keep my name out if it when you start cleaning up.'

'Thanks for the word,' Loman said with a nod. 'I'll remember what you've told me, and I'll keep your name out of it.'

Shaw nodded, turned, and retreated into the shadows. Loman gazed after him; digesting the information he had been given. He led his horse outside and swung into the saddle, wondering what to make of the little liveryman. Riding along the street, he paused outside the law office, intending to pass on to Sorgan the information he had received, but then decided against it, aware that he was riding out to Double H and could make his own assessment of what was happening.

He rode on to the front of the hotel and found Kate Hesp standing on the sidewalk, talking animatedly to her two hired hands. Three saddle-horses were tied to a hitch rack nearby. From the attitudes of Jackson and Emmet, Loman figured they were being reprimanded. He sat his mount and gazed around the shadowed street, and Kate cut short her tirade when she saw him.

'OK. Let's forget it now,' she said sternly. 'But there better not be any more of it. We'll ride back to the ranch and you two can start doing the job you get paid for. One of you ride ahead and the other can bring up the rear. There could be trouble after what's happened in town tonight, so keep your eyes lifting.'

She mounted and rode in beside Loman, her face shadowed in the dim light pervading the town. Loman wondered what was driving her and reached the conclusion that she was afraid for her father. He chewed on that while they rode out of town. Curly Jackson spurred several yards ahead and settled into a steady lope while Fred Emmet dropped behind a similar distance and followed steadily. They left town and hit the open trail, heading north-west.

A crescent moon gave silvery light to their surroundings while playing hide and seek with the small, fleecy clouds drifting fast across the night sky. Shadows clung to the ground in unexpected places, causing distant objects to look deceptive. The wind was blowing into their faces, bringing scents and smells from a thousand miles of prairie, plains, woods and mountains. There was little to disturb the heavy silence of the trail; only the creaking of saddle leather and the dull thud of hoofs.

Kate was silent for some time after they had left town, and Loman was content to ride quietly, hoping that she would begin to open up about what was on her mind. He could tell she was troubled, and could not help but wonder why she would not take Sorgan into her confidence. If she and the sheriff were due to be married in the near future then there should be no secrets between them.

They travelled a couple of miles before Kate broke the silence. When she spoke her tone was brittle, sounding as if she were biting off her words.

'I don't know what you must be thinking, Ward. I could tell back there in the office that you didn't believe a word I was saying about what happened in that alley.'

'And neither did James,' Loman responded.

'I couldn't tell him the truth. He would have pulled his gun and gone through the town like an avenging angel.'

'The truth will have to come out before long, and James may find himself at a disadvantage when he does start to clean up, if you don't set him straight with the facts.'

'This situation wouldn't have arisen if Curly and Fred had done their job properly,' she complained. 'And I don't want my father to know about that business in town so please don't mention it. You wouldn't understand, but Dad has plenty of trouble on his plate without being burdened with mine, and he's not well.'

'I might be able to understand if you took me into your confidence,' Loman said firmly. 'There's nothing worse than being left in the dark with instructions to follow the play by instinct. I can't help you at all if I have to wear a blindfold. I know that Hub Slattery is handling some rustling, and Double H has been raided amongst others, but the deal goes much deeper than that, and what happened in town tonight is a part of it.'

'How do you know that much?' Kate's face was a

pale blur as she gazed at him. 'Did James tell you anything?'

'James doesn't appear to know anything,' he responded, 'and you're making a big mistake by not telling him the truth. What is happening that makes you think you can handle trouble better alone?'

'You wouldn't understand,' she said miserably.

'I'd have a better chance of understanding if I had the knowledge you refuse to give. Anything you say to me wouldn't go an inch further. If you can't talk about your troubles then tell me what your dad has got heaped on his plate. All ranchers have problems; that's the way of life in the West. If it isn't cattle prices then it's drought or rustlers. There's never any end to it. But I think there's something more than that on this range. Take a chance and tell me about it, because you'll never beat it on your own.'

Loman paused to give her time to think over his words, and silence closed in around them. She rode steadily, glancing around, but he knew his words had given her cause to question her attitude. He did not relax his alertness, and when an orange flash split the darkness off to their right he lunged out of his saddle, and was dragging Kate with him before the report of a rifle shot hammered and echoed across the range. He hit the ground hard, but not before he heard the crackle of a bullet passing closely by his right ear.

He pushed Kate down as she tried to rise, and drew his pistol as he sprang up. The night was suddenly split by several guns firing, and he dropped flat instantly.

THREE

Having ordered Kate to remain where she was, Loman crawled off to the right before getting to one knee. He saw gun flashes splitting the shadows about fifty yards from the trail and estimated that four guns were shooting at them. Jackson and Emmet were replying to the attack with their pistols, and strings of echoes were sent hurtling across the range. A rifle cracked close by, and Loman turned his head to see Kate standing behind her mount, firing a Winchester across the saddle.

He went to his horse and snatched up the reins before swinging into the saddle. He holstered his pistol and drew his Winchester from its saddle boot. He cocked it.

'Don't shoot me,' he called to Kate. 'I'm going over there to see who's causing the rumpus.'

He touched spurs to his horse and sent the animal towards the cluster of guns firing at them. He dropped his reins across the neck of the horse and used both hands to work his rifle, sending a rapid stream of shots into the thick of their assailants.

Curly Jackson loomed up from the left and moved to Loman's side, and Emmet ceased firing and hastened to catch up with them.

Loman ignored the lead that was tossed at them. He kept firing at the flaring gun flashes as he galloped forward, and such was his marksmanship that two of the attackers soon dropped out of the fight. The shooting stopped before they reached the position, and when they eventually halted they could hear the sound of rapidly retiring riders galloping into the anonymity of the shadowed range.

Two horses were standing with trailing reins at the spot where the shooting had started. Loman stepped down from his saddle, slid his rifle into its boot and drew his pistol.

'That sure was some shooting!' Jackson acknowledged. 'I didn't hit a thing, but you did. I hope you're gonna stick around here now the trouble is coming into the open. Sorgan is a good man with a gun, but he ain't stepping out of line. He's playing a waiting game, hoping things will shape his way instead of getting out and tracking down the bad men.'

'Let's find the two I did hit,' Loman said. 'Cover me while I look for them. They may be wounded and waiting for a clear shot at us.'

Jackson cocked his gun. Loman looked around, his own weapon ready. He saw a dark figure stretched out nearby and walked towards it, covering it as he closed in. There was no movement, and he dropped to one knee beside the man and used his left hand to feel for signs of life. His fingers found a patch of blood on the man's shirt-front when he felt for a heart beat, but found no movement. The man was dead.

'The other one is here,' Jackson called. 'He's dead. Took a slug through the face, it looks like.'

Loman crossed to where Jackson was standing and saw the upturned face of another dead man. He glanced around as Emmet rode up, and the sound of Kate coming towards them was loud in the background.

'Strike a match and take a look at these two,' Loman suggested. 'See if you know either of them.'

Emmet dropped to one knee and there was the scrape of a match. A tiny flame flickered briefly and then was extinguished by the strong breeze.

'Well?' Loman demanded impatiently.

'I don't know him,' Emmet said. 'He's a stranger to me.'

'And to me,' Jackson said. 'Let's take a look at the other one. They can't all be strangers operating around here.'

Both men went across to the second ambusher to check him. Kate arrived and slid out of her saddle.

'Did you get some of them?' she demanded.

'Two out of four,' Loman said tensely.

'This one is a stranger as well,' Jackson called.

'Hey, it looks like a horse is down over there,' Emmet observed.

Loman swung around, his keen eyes narrowing. He saw an indistinct shadow on the ground some twenty yards away and went forward at a run, followed by the two cowhands. They found a horse lying on its side, flanks heaving, its laboured breathing whistling through a bullet hole in one of its lungs. The animal lifted its head at their approach, and then let it flop to the ground. Loman drew his gun and fired a single shot into the animal's brain. He listened grimly to the echoes scattering to the horizon.

'Take a look at it,' he advised. 'You might know it by sight.'

Emmet struck a match and they inspected the carcass. The match flickered out and Jackson struck another one to take a second look at the stricken horse.

'I got the feeling I've seen this animal around plenty,' he said musingly. 'Brown face with a white muzzle and two white fetlocks at the front. We've seen this horse around town some, Fred, and sometimes on the range. Thing is, who rides it?'

'Yeah,' Emmet said slowly, shaking his head as he considered. He stiffened suddenly. 'Hey, you know who rides this horse – Wes Slattery!'

'Hell if you ain't right.' Jackson struck another match and shielded it against the breeze with his hands. He looked over the carcass more closely, and when the match expired he straightened. 'You got it, Fred. That's Wes Slattery's horse. But what's it doing here, huh? I got Wes pegged as reckless punk, but I don't figger him for an ambusher. Do you reckon the horse was stole from Wes? HS say they's been losing some steers; perhaps the horse was taken as well.'

'We know what it was doing here,' Emmet replied grimly. 'One of the four men shooting at us was riding it, and I don't need to be told who it was. Wes Slattery is always mixed up in anything bad going on around this range. I reckon he's afoot out there somewhere, trying to put distance between himself and us. There sure is hell gonna bust loose when the boss learns about this. It's open war and the Slatterys are behind it, like we always figured. But they've gone too far this time.'

'We are not going to tell my dad anything,' Kate said as she came up to them.

'You can't keep a thing like this a secret,' Loman said softly. 'There are two dead men here who have to be accounted for. We need to get at the truth of what's going on, and ensure that it doesn't happen again.'

'Double H will take care of its own troubles as and when they come up,' Kate said. 'Come on, you two. Mount up and let's get on to the ranch. What are you going to do, Ward?'

'I don't know off-hand. I'm new to this law-dealing business. Thinking about it, I reckon I better ride back to town and talk to James. Are you two sure that dead horse belongs to Wes Slattery?'

'Without a doubt,' Jackson said.

'Then I'll ride back to town,' Loman decided. 'With any luck I'll be out at Double H some time tomorrow, if that is all right with you, Kate?'

'Sure. Whenever you can make it. I'll tell Dad to expect you.'

She turned to her horse and swung into the saddle, and the two cowhands did likewise. Loman watched them ride off into the night until they had vanished in the shadows, then fetched his horse and mounted. He rode back to the trail and headed for Coldwater, his thoughts chaotic as he tried to come to terms with what was happening around him.

The town looked to be asleep by the time he reached the outskirts, and he saw only a few lamps alight along the main street. He rode to the law office, passing the saloon, which was still busy, and frowned when he came upon two Conestoga wagons, their teams removed, parked one behind the other in front of the general store, which was closed. A man armed with a rifle detached himself from the deep shadows surrounding one of the wagons and gazed intently at Loman as he passed by.

Loman dismounted in front of the law office, tried the door and found it locked. He looked around as a voice hailed him from the shadowed sidewalk, and recognized Sorgan's voice.

'Hey, Ward, I thought you were riding out to Double H.'

'Something changed my mind, James.' Loman waited until he was joined by the sheriff.

'I've just finished my evening round,' Sorgan said. 'The town is quiet. So what brought you back on the jump?'

Loman explained and Sorgan whistled through his teeth.

'Are you sure about that horse being Wes Slattery's?'

'Jackson and Emmet were dead sure.'

'Uhuh. Well, we can soon get to the truth about that. I saw Wes coming into town about five minutes ago. He was riding double with a stranger. He went straight into the saloon. Let's go talk to him.'

They went along the sidewalk to the saloon.

'What are those two wagons doing in front of the store?' Loman asked. 'They usually stay outside of town. Are they settlers? I saw a man guarding them.'

'I checked them over when they pulled in. There's a party of half a dozen men with an ex-army major Oliver Bracknell in command. He reckons they're on some kind of government business – surveying or the like. Says there is a dispute about boundaries north and west of here that he's got to check out. They'll be gone on their way by first light. They even got a special deputy US marshal riding with them.'

'That's unusual,' Loman commented.

'Yeah.' Sorgan chuckled. 'I'd give a lot to know what Bracknell has got on his mind. They were loading up with supplies just before the store closed for the night, and it looked like they was getting set to take care of a whole army, the stuff that was bought.'

They entered the saloon and Loman remained at Sorgan's left elbow as they paused on the threshold. There were more than a dozen men inside, and Sorgan glanced at Loman.

'That's the major's party over there at those two tables in the corner. Wes Slattery is along the bar. He's the one wearing the red shirt. Let's brace him and see which way he jumps.'

Loman checked out the newcomers seated at two tables, looking for familiar faces. He saw only strangers, and had a moment's disquiet when he spotted a shield-shaped law badge on the shirt-front of a big, broad-shouldered man with a rugged face that looked as if it had been hewn out of granite. He was aware that all of the men at the two tables looked up at the sound of the batwings opening, and cold gazes were directed at the sheriff and himself.

Sorgan went directly towards a tall, slim man standing at the far end of the bar, and a glance at him was enough to establish his identity in Loman's mind because he was the image of Leo Slattery. Wes Slattery was dark-haired and handsome, around twenty-four, and there was an air about him that bespoke of a restless nature, which was bolstered by an arrogant glint in his brown eyes. He was wearing crossed gun belts around his narrow waist which contained matched, pearl-handled .45 Colt pistols.

'Howdy, Wes.' Sorgan paused before the youngster. 'When did you ride in?'

'A few minutes ago. What's it to you?' Slattery's tone contained a challenge and an invitation, which Sorgan ignored with a faint smile.

'Where's your horse?' the sheriff continued.

'My horse? What makes you ask that partickler question? I was about to look you up to report that it was stolen from our ranch during the night. Not that I expect you or anyone else to find it for me, the way the law operates in this county.' Slattery grinned insolently as if he had made a huge joke, and dropped his right hand to the butt of the pistol on his right hip. 'We lost some stock, too, about three hundred head taken off our home range clean as a whistle. Them rustlers are getting plenty open about their crooked business.'

'Your horse has been found.' Sorgan spoke in a matter-of-fact tone that revealed nothing of his feelings. 'Come along to the office and we'll go into details.'

Slattery stiffened and straightened, pushing himself away from the bar, his expression changing as his manner hardened.

'What gives?' he demanded. 'Are you arresting me?'

'You've sure got a guilty conscience,' Sorgan replied smoothly. 'What's on your mind, Wes? What have you done that you think I might want you for?'

'Hell, you're always so tricky. What's on *your* mind?'

'Come along to the office and I'll tell you.' Sorgan's tone had changed to encompass a grating quality that moved Slattery into gripping the butt of his gun. His eyes narrowed, and he inflated his chest with a deep breath as he teetered on the brink of action. 'Don't even think of pulling a gun,' Sorgan advised. 'You'd never clear leather, punk! Lift your hands, and make it quick, or you'll need the attention of the undertaker. It's your choice.'

Slattery froze and his narrowed eyes opened wide as he relaxed and grinned.

'Who's been stepping on your toes, Sheriff?' he demanded. 'Heck, I wouldn't dream of going up against you. I'm all for law and order. Sure I'll step along to the law office. My old man has warned me to show you badge-toters all the respect you're entitled to from law-abiding folks.'

'Cut the gab or you'll be parting from your front

teeth,' Sorgan said quietly. 'Take out your pistols one at a time and lay them on the bar. Don't even think of resisting or you'll wind up on your face in the sawdust. I warned you the last time we met that you better mind your manners when you come to town.'

'What have I said that's wrong?' Slattery demanded.

Sorgan's right hand moved with the speed of a striking snake and his pistol appeared in his hand, the muzzle digging into Slattery's belly.

'Get 'em up and cut the cackle. I don't like the sound of your voice, you skunk, so you'll keep quiet if you know what's good for you.'

Slattery raised his hands, his eyes glittering with repressed emotion. Sorgan lifted the youngster's right-hand gun from its holster and handed it to Loman.

'Take his second gun as well, Ward,' he said, and Loman complied. 'Now let's go along to my office and we'll get down to business. You've got everyone in the saloon looking at you, Slattery, which is what you wanted, huh?'

'I don't know what this is about,' Slattery said. 'You're getting heavy-handed, Sheriff, and all I've done is had my horse stole.'

Sorgan grasped the youngster's shoulder and thrust him towards the batwings, his pistol jammed against Slattery's spine. The swing-doors were pushed open just before Slattery reached them and a big man entered the saloon, stopping almost in mid-stride when he saw Slattery bearing down on him with his hands raised above his head.

Loman found himself looking into a pair of the coldest blue eyes he had ever seen. The newcomer was dressed in a brown store-suit of very good quality. His jacket was open to reveal a brown waistcoat with a pure-white shirt underneath. His feet were encased in highly polished brown shoes which shone despite the film of dust coating them. He was wearing a cartridge belt with a pistol holstered on his right hip.

'Something wrong, Sheriff?' he demanded in a cultivated voice that was vibrant with a big Northern-city accent – flat and hard. He stepped aside as Slattery continued to the door.

'Nothing I can't handle, Major,' Sorgan replied. 'Ward, this is Major Bracknell. He's with those wagons parked in front of the store. Ward Loman, my deputy, Major. See him if you have any problems around town.'

'Thank you, Sheriff, but I have a good crew with me who can handle just about any eventuality. I've even brought along my own lawman.' Bracknell smiled and went on across the saloon to where his men were seated.

Slattery shouldered through the batwings and went on along the sidewalk with Sorgan and Loman following closely. Once inside the law office, Sorgan pushed Slattery into a seat before the desk and stood over him menacingly.

'You better give it to me straight, Wes,' he said harshly. 'I ain't in no mood for games. I can easy check your story about having your horse stole, so quit that line and come up with the truth.'

'I told you the truth,' Slattery protested. 'I can't do

no more than that. What do you think I'm guilty of? I ain't done a blame thing that's wrong.'

'You wouldn't recognize innocence if it came up and smacked you in the mouth,' Sorgan snapped. 'You were born guilty, Slattery. Now open up, or you'll wish you'd never been spawned. You've just come into town, and you were riding double with a stranger, so tell me what you were doing an hour gone?'

'Been hunting those rustlers all day. Tracks led off into the west from HS. Mighty bad country out that way, and when them steers hit hard ground we lost tracks. Hunted around all afternoon for fresh sign and didn't find a thing. We got back to the spread late afternoon, and I came into town for a couple of drinks and some fun. The horse I was riding went lame, and I got a ride in the rest of the way with one of our outfit.'

'Who rode with you today?' Sorgan asked.

Slattery shrugged. 'Some of our outfit, who else?'

'I'll check on your story.' Sorgan picked up the cell keys. 'You're gonna stay put in jail until I've cleared you.'

'Hey, that ain't fair, Sheriff. What for you need to lock me up? I ain't going anywhere. You can always find me when you want me. I got myself some fun pegged out for tonight.'

'Get up and empty your pockets on the desk,' Sorgan rapped. 'I've heard just about all I can take of your voice so shut your mouth or I'll shut it for you.'

Slattery gazed into Sorgan's face, noted the degree of resolution in the sheriff's eyes, and sighed long and hard. He opened his mouth to speak and then thought better of the action and closed it again. He turned out his pockets, then held his hands wide of his body, smiling insolently, his manner spiked with defiance.

'That's all,' he said.

Sorgan pushed him towards the door leading into the cells. Loman waited by the desk until Sorgan returned, rattling the bunch of keys. Sitting down at the desk, the sheriff shook his head.

'Ward, I don't like the way this business is settling around Kate and her pa. I got no idea what is going on, but trouble has been sneaking up on Double H for some time. I'm gonna have to ride out there and look around for myself. I hate to drop you in at the deep end like this, but I'd like you to stick around town and keep an eye on things while I'm gone. It's asking a lot of you, being a stranger, but knowing you, I'd say you can hold up your end in any situation. Just keep an eye open for law breakers – you shouldn't have any real problems in that respect around town. I'll be back soon as I can make it.'

'Sure. I reckon I can handle it. The trouble is, none of your townsfolk knows me from Adam. They're gonna get a shock come morning when they find a stranger representing their law.'

'Yeah. You're right. I'd better take you around town and introduce you to some of the town council. There'll be no problems if they know you by sight.'

They left the office and went along the street. Sorgan led the way into the hotel, paused in the doorway of the private bar and signalled to a short, fat man to join them.

'This is Sam Brewster, who owns the hotel, Ward,' Sorgan introduced. 'Sam, this is Ward Loman, an old friend of mine. He rode into town earlier, not knowing I was here, and I took him on as a deputy. I'm leaving town for a couple of days, and Ward will be around to handle the law. If you have any problems while I'm away then call on Ward.'

'Glad to know you, Loman.' Brewster smiled. 'Any friend of the sheriff is OK by me. You've showed up at the right time. All the signs are that we've got some trouble brewing. Come and have a drink.'

'Thanks, Sam,' Sorgan interrupted. 'We're pushed right now. Later, huh?'

'Sure. Good luck, Loman. You look like you can handle yourself, and it could get very tough around here before long.'

They took their leave and Sorgan led the way to the general store, which was in darkness. They entered an alley that had a lantern burning over a doorway about half-way along its length and Sorgan knocked. The door was opened by a tall, thin man whose bald head shone in the lamplight.

'Sorry to trouble you, Frank. I want you to meet my new deputy,' Sorgan introduced, and Loman found himself being regarded by suspicious brown eyes. 'Ward Loman, meet Frank Mason. Frank is the town mayor. I want you two to know each other while I'm out of town. Ward is a good friend of mine, Frank. You can trust him up to the hilt.'

Loman shook hands with Mason.

'It's about time you took on an extra deputy,

James,' Mason said. 'The town council was talking about that earlier this evening. We're getting mighty worried about the way trouble is growing. It'll need a firm hand to bring matters under control. You'll have to do something about Wes and Charlie Slattery. Get them minding the law and most of the trouble around here should disappear.'

'I agree those two are a problem, but they ain't the whole of it.' Sorgan shook his head. 'We just put Wes Slattery behind bars, though I don't expect to be able to hold him long. Anyway, you'll know Ward by sight around town. He's a good man and you can trust him.'

'You've jailed Wes?' Mason smiled and his tone became easier. 'Mind you, it's not before time.'

'You know I got to act within the letter of the law,' Sorgan said. 'If I had my way I'd run those Slattery brothers clear out of the county.'

'What's Wes been up to now?' Mason enquired.

'He's partly the reason why I've got to leave town. I'll bring you up to date when I get back. See you around, Frank. I need to get moving pronto.'

They left the store and Sorgan paused on the sidewalk to look around the deserted street. The two unhitched wagons blocked their vision somewhat, and Loman was preoccupied with trying to assemble his impressions of the town. He could sense an air of disquiet in Coldwater, and wondered what was behind it. A loud voice calling a challenge disturbed his mental processes, and as he looked around a rifle shot crashed and the flash of a long gun split the shadows between the two wagons.

Sorgan reacted instantly, running forward, drawing his gun, and Loman went with him, ready for action. It seemed that the trouble, whatever it was, had at last broken loose.

FOUR

A figure detached itself from the shadows around the second wagon and ran a couple of steps along the street before pitching face down in the dust. The echoes of the shot racketed across the town and a dog barked frenziedly at the disturbance. Loman stayed beside Sorgan, and they halted quickly when a hoarse voice challenged them from the back of the first wagon.

'I'm the sheriff,' Sorgan replied. 'What's going on?'

'I'm guarding these wagons, and someone was trying to steal from that one. He started to run so I shot him.' The man holding the rifle emerged from the back of the nearest wagon, muzzle covering Sorgan and Loman.

'Point that Winchester someplace else,' Sorgan rapped, and then reached out and snatched the long gun from the man's hand. 'What's your name, mister?'

'Cal Frazee. I work for Major Bracknell, and I got strict orders on how to act, so talk to the major if you got any problems.'

'I don't like guns being fired around town,' Sorgan said icily, 'and the major ain't got the right to tell anyone to shoot a man for just nosing round a wagon.'

'This is government property.' Frazee was a big man, muscular, and obviously handy with a gun. His voice held a note of disdain and Sorgan reacted to it.

'I don't care whose property it is.' Sorgan went forward to where the inert figure was lying and dropped to one knee to check it out. He cursed, and then straightened. 'It's Joel Bender, the town drunk, and he's dead,' he said. 'You're in a lot of trouble, Frazee. Joel wouldn't steal a red cent. He was probably looking for a place to put his head down for the night.'

'I was obeying orders,' Frazee said doggedly. 'You better call the major. He'll square things.'

'He can try, but I'm sticking you in jail all the same. The office is that way.' Sorgan pointed along the sidewalk. 'Let's get down there before a crowd gathers.'

They moved on, and met a couple of townsmen coming along the street.

'What happened, Sheriff?' one demanded.

'Joel Bender's been shot. He's dead. Go tell Pete Ives to remove the body and I'll see him later about the burial.'

They had to pass the saloon, where a group of men were standing in front of the batwings. Loman recognized Major Bracknell in the forefront, and the ex-officer barred Sorgan's way when he recognized Frazee.

'What's happened, Sheriff?' Bracknell demanded. 'I heard a shot. Have you arrested Frazee?'

'I've got to take a statement from him before I decide what's going to happen. He had no right to shoot a man who wasn't armed and didn't pose a threat to him.'

'Frazee was acting under my orders.' Bracknell's voice cracked like a whip.

'Then perhaps I ought to arrest you along with him,' Sorgan said firmly. 'This is law business, Major, so stay out of it. On your way, Frazee. I've got other things to do tonight before I can call it a day.'

They went on to the law office, and Loman noted that the major did not follow them. Frazee refused to say anything more when questioned, and Sorgan searched him, then put him in a cell. The sheriff's face was grim when he returned to the office.

'Ward, I got a feeling I'd better stick around town with this trouble,' he said. 'My personal problems will have to wait. It wouldn't be fair to leave you here alone. You ride out to Double H tomorrow, huh?'

'Sure. It won't be a problem.' Loman sat down on the chair in front of the desk. 'It looks like your big trouble is coming to a head.'

'I've seen the signs for weeks, and I thought I could handle it with a fast draw, but it's getting complicated. What's the major got in those wagons he's so all-fired anxious to keep secret? There wasn't any call for Frazee to shoot old Joel. And there'll be hell to pay tomorrow when Hub Slattery hears I've got Wes behind bars and comes to get the reason. I'm gonna be up to my neck in it for sure. Hub's got a couple of real salty gunhands on his pay-roll, and I wouldn't put it past him to turn them loose on me.'

'Maybe I should stick around town for a couple of days,' Loman suggested. 'It looks like the action is gonna happen here, not at Double H.'

The door of the office was thrust open noisily and Loman turned quickly, his hand dropping to the butt of his gun. A tall, thin man entered, and Loman caught the glint of a law badge on the newcomer's shirt front.

'What's going on, James?' he demanded. 'I heard a shot, and just saw Joel Bender dead on the street.'

'Where have you been all evening, Al?' Sorgan's tone revealed impatience. 'You're never around when I need you.'

'I've been keeping an ear to the ground like you told me to.' Al's dark gaze was upon Loman, and his eyes narrowed when he saw the deputy badge on Loman's chest.

'This is Ward Loman, an old friend of mine,' Sorgan introduced. 'Meet Al Donovan, Ward. He ain't no great shakes as a deputy, but he's the best I could find until you came along.'

'Glad to know you, Loman.' Donovan nodded and grinned, but there was hostility in his brown eyes. He was tall and slim, looked to be in his middle-forties, and wore a Remington .44 in a low-slung holster on his left side.

'Howdy,' Loman greeted.

'I'd leave you here with Al, but I can't trust him to

do anything right,' Sorgan said. 'I keep him on as a deputy because he's the mayor's nephew. But even that excuse is wearing thin these days. What have you learned today about the local situation, Al?'

'There's nothing going on that I can find,' Donovan replied. 'I don't know where you keep getting these rumours from about trouble acomin'.'

'Did you pick up anything about Major Bracknell and his outfit?' Sorgan persisted.

'Nary a thing. They're a close-mouthed bunch, and they ain't friendly neither. That deputy US marshal riding with them is something else, and all. Real prickly cuss with no sense of humour. Looks like he's ready to pull his gun at the drop of a hat. I reckon he's a hardcase with no regard for the law, but he's living on his nerves. He seems jumpy as a two-year-old filly. His name is Ben Lacey.'

'You better keep a close eye on that bunch, Al,' Sorgan decided. 'Follow them when they leave town, and check on what they do. The major says they're gonna pull out tomorrow. And don't let them catch sight of you, just in case. I got feelings about Bracknell, and they ain't good.'

'I'll go off duty now.' Donovan had a lazy grin on his face. 'See you around, Loman. Don't work too hard.'

'He won't if he follows your example,' Sorgan said testily.

Donovan shrugged and departed. Loman shook his head, suspecting there was more to Donovan than showed.

'He ain't too bad when you get to know him,'

Sorgan said. 'He'll nose around until he finds something. But I've made up my mind to stick around town so you ride out to Double H tomorrow. It will set my mind at rest. Kate will be safe in your company.'

'I'll hit the trail at dawn. Just give me directions for finding Double H and you can leave it to me.'

'Come and look at the map of the county over there.' Sorgan walked around the desk. He waited for Loman to join him and explained the geography of Tate County. Loman made a mental note of the area he would be operating in and turned away. 'Have you got yourself a bed for the night?' Sorgan concluded.

'I haven't had time to consider that.' Loman smiled wryly. 'Life has been hectic since I hit town.'

'I got a shack at the end of the street.' Sorgan produced a key and held it out. 'It ain't much, but it goes with the job. I won't be using it tonight, that's for sure. I'll be too busy here. So you're welcome to bed down there. It's the last place on the other side of the street going south; right opposite the stable. When you get to Double H tomorrow have a word with Henry Hesp. He'll tell you what he thinks is going on out his way, and anything you get from him will be the truth. You can trust to that.'

'OK. I'll turn in now and hit the trail at dawn tomorrow.' Loman took the key and dropped it into a breast pocket.

'Thanks, Ward.' Sorgan grinned. 'It's good to see you again. We had some high old times together, huh? I'm sorry it ain't quieter around here, but once this business is under control I'll make your visit something to remember.'

Loman smiled and departed. He walked along the sidewalk towards the stable and crossed the street at an angle, his thoughts filled with the problems besetting Sorgan, and did not envy the sheriff his job. In the back of his mind was the thought that he should not be getting too closely involved in local trouble or he might have difficulty disentangling himself. All he wanted in Tate County was a sight of Leo Slattery and, when Leo was taken, he could fade back into the wilderness of the range and resume his secretive life.

There was a lantern burning over the entrance to the stable on the opposite side of the street and Loman saw the sheriff's shack standing alone beyond the end of the sidewalk. Shadows were dense around the shack, and Loman moved in silently, his gaze probing for movement. He produced Sorgan's key and fumbled for the lock, his shadow covering the door. Moving a pace to the left, he bent at the waist to look more closely for the keyhole, and heard a thud as a heavy object struck the door close to his head.

His reaction was such that he dropped to his right knee and drew his pistol without realizing he had done so. He caught a glimpse of a dark figure at the left-hand corner of the shack and covered it.

'Hold it,' he rapped. 'I got a bead on you.'

The figure turned to run for deeper shadows, and Loman fired instinctively, narrowing his gaze against the flash that erupted from his muzzle. The figure dropped instantly and lay still. Loman stood up, listening to the echoes fleeing across the peaceful town.

He checked his surroundings as full silence returned, looked at the big knife stuck in the door of the shack, and then walked towards the motionless figure lying in the dust. Satisfied that he was alone, he bent to remove a pistol from a holster before placing a hand on the inert man's chest. There was no heartbeat. He straightened and stood waiting for the curious of the town's populace to arrive.

The sound of running footsteps along the street, drawing rapidly nearer, alerted Loman, and he caught a glimpse of a man approaching.

'Declare yourself,' he challenged.

'Sorgan.' The reply came quickly, and Loman lowered the hammer of his gun and slid the weapon back into its holster. 'What happened, Ward?'

Loman explained tersely, and the sheriff uttered a curse as he dropped to one knee beside the dead man. He struck a match and held it close to an upturned face. Loman saw bearded features before darkness returned, and Sorgan regained his feet, cursing freely.

'What in hell is going on around here?' Sorgan was agitated. 'This man is a stranger. I've never set eyes on him before. Why in hell would he wanta stick a knife in you? Do you know him, Ward?'

'No. He's a stranger. And he wasn't out to get me.' Loman spoke quietly. 'It's your shack, James. You must have been the target.'

Sorgan remained silent for a moment, evidently

thinking over the import of Loman's words, and then sighed heavily.

'You're right, of course.' Sorgan glanced around. Footsteps thudded along the street. He went to the door of the shack and pulled out the knife. 'This is the only evidence we've got. I must talk to Amos Shaw. He always seems to know what's going on in town. This guy didn't walk here from where ever he's from. He must have a horse someplace.' He stuck the knife in his belt. 'Let's go talk to Shaw.'

Several men were approaching, and Sorgan called to them. They were townsmen, and the sheriff sent one to fetch the undertaker. Amos Shaw was coming across the street from the stable. Someone struck a match to view the dead man's features, and Shaw craned forward to see.

'This feller was in the stable about an hour ago,' the liveryman said. 'Him and another. I heard them talking. This one told the other that he had a job to do, and the other said he would wait in the saloon until it was done. So this was what he had in mind, huh? He was planning to kill you, Sheriff.'

'Why didn't you report to me when you heard what was said, Amos?' Sorgan demanded.

'I had no idea what sort of a job he was planning,' Shaw protested. 'Anyway, you know my policy. I don't let on about what I hear in the barn. If I talked about some of the things that are said I'd wind up with a knife in my back.'

'Would you recognize the other man?' Sorgan asked.

'Sure would. You want I should point him out to you, Sheriff?'

'If it ain't against your policy,' Sorgan replied.

Shaw set off along the street and Sorgan and Loman followed closely. Shaw peered through a front window into the saloon, and then turned away.

'He's in there all right,' he said. 'Tall feller wearing a black Stetson and a blue shirt. I'll get back to my barn before you take him. I wouldn't want anyone to know I put the finger on him.'

Sorgan shouldered open the batwings as the liveryman departed, and Loman was close behind the sheriff as he crossed the threshold. Loman glanced around and saw that Major Bracknell and his men had departed. He was still wondering about the major's set-up when Sorgan confronted the tall stranger. The sheriff lifted the man's pistol from his holster, and stepped back a pace when the man swung round to face him.

'What's your name, feller?' Sorgan demanded.

'What's goin' on?' the man countered. His dark eyes narrowed when he saw the law star on Sorgan's chest, and then his gaze flickered to Loman. He shook his head and set the glass he was holding back on the bar. 'The local law, huh?' he said. 'So what's this all about? Is it against the law in this town for a stranger to get himself a couple of drinks? I'm minding my own business, and I ain't causing any trouble.'

'Mebbe you ain't, but the man you rode into town with an hour ago is lying dead in the street. He tried to knife a lawman but didn't make it.'

'Hey, I rode into town alone,' the man protested.

'I don't know where you got your information from, but I just got in from Mexico.'

'I got a witness says he saw you and this other feller talking together in the stable. You came along here while your sidekick went off to do a job. Now tell me your name.'

'I'm Ike Taylor. Like I said, I just got in from Mexico, and I rode alone. You got me mixed up with someone else.'

'Let's talk about it some more down at the jail,' Sorgan said. 'Hold your hands up while I search you.'

The man shrugged and raised his hands. Sorgan searched him, and then motioned to the door.

'Let's go,' he said, 'and you better use the time between here and the jail to think about telling the truth.'

They left the saloon. When they reached the law office Loman paused.

'You can manage without me, James,' he said. 'I'm gonna turn in now, and I'll use the stable. There might be others in town who want to get at you, and your shack is the likeliest place for them to start looking.'

Sorgan grinned but his eyes held a grim expression.

'Check with me in the morning before you ride out, Ward,' he replied.

Loman went to the stable and found Amos Shaw in his dusty office. The liveryman's face was pale and he seemed agitated. A double-barrelled Greener 12-gauge shotgun lay across the near corner of his desk, the twin muzzles covering the door. His right hand was on the stock of the weapon when Loman saw him.

'I don't know what this town is coming to,' Shaw said when he recognized Loman. He sat back in his seat and lifted his hand from the shotgun. 'Strangers coming in and trying to kill the sheriff! Just what is going on?'

'I want you to point out the horses those two rode in on,' Loman said. Shaw got up from the desk, picked up a lantern, and walked into the barn.

'These two.' He paused before two animals in an open stall. 'They came in together, told me they would be riding out in the morning, and went out to the street together. That's their gear on that rail – saddles, saddle-bags, and all.'

Loman opened the saddle-bags, hoping to find some clue to the identity of the two men, but found nothing significant. He gave up on the search.

'Mind if I hit the sack in your loft?' he asked. 'When I pound my ear I like to know I'm not likely to be murdered in my sleep.'

'Sure you can. Be a comfort to know you're up there if I get any more customers like the last two.' Shaw laughed as if he had made a joke.

Loman fetched his blanket roll from the stall where his horse was stabled and climbed the loft ladder to settle down in sweet-smelling hay. Within minutes he was asleep, and lay quietly until he awoke, according to habit, as the greyness of dawn stole into the barn.

Shaw was in his office, and looked as if he had been there all night. He seemed to have taken root on the chair behind the desk, and grinned tiredly as he pointed to a coffee-pot standing on a corner of the desk.

'Just made that coffee,' he said. 'Help yourself to a cup, son. It'll set you up for breakfast. You're an early riser like me, huh?'

Loman nodded and took a cup of coffee. He sat on a corner of the desk to drink it, and questioned Shaw closely in an attempt to elicit more information. Shaw was ill at ease, and his manner was such that Loman gave up and went to the eating-house for breakfast.

After a meal he walked along to the law office. He noticed that Bracknell's two wagons were gone from the front of the store. He gazed around the deserted street, wondering about the major's operations. He heard boots pounding the sidewalk and looked round to see Sorgan coming towards him.

'Bracknell and his bunch pulled out around three a.m. this morning,' Sorgan said. 'When the major said last night that he wanted to make an early start he certainly meant it. I didn't cotton to him, Ward, and I got a nose for trouble. I wanta know what he's up to with those two wagons and a deputy US marshal tagging along. If they know anything at all about surveying then I'll eat my saddle, stirrups and all.'

'Did you learn anything from Ike Taylor about his knife-throwing sidekick?' Loman asked.

Sorgan shook his head. 'He's still denying all knowledge of that business. I searched the body and found nothing that would identify it, which is suspicious in itself. Most men have got some identification on them, unless they're up to no good. Donovan rode out behind Bracknell's wagons, and I sure hope he don't make any mistakes and get himself took by the major. That bunch don't take any prisoners, it looks like. Have you had breakfast yet?'

'Yep. I'm riding out to Double H now. Is there anything you want me to do?'

'It'll be enough if you talk to Henry Hesp. In the past he's near jawed my ears off with his suspicions of what's going on around the county. If you get the chance, drop by HS and tell Hub Slattery that his boy Wes is behind bars. It'll also give you the chance to see if Leo has showed up yet. And that's about it, Ward, except that I'm real worried about Kate. I got a hunch that someone is about to put pressure on Henry by grabbing Kate, or something like that.'

'Leave it with me,' Loman said. 'While I'm at the ranch I'll stick closer to that gal than her shadow. See you around, James.'

'Sure, and I appreciate your help, Ward. I'm up a gum tree right now. This game is too deep for me to work out, and if I don't get on top of it soon then I might be sorry at the way it turns out when slugs start flying. All the signs are there, and it scares the hell out of me.'

Loman nodded and went on to the stable. Ten minutes later he was riding north out of town, and cantering along the trail to Double H with the sun glinting on the law badge pinned to his shirt. He watched his surroundings as he travelled, his caution ingrained by hard experience. He could see the wheel tracks of Bracknell's two wagons heading in the direction he was following, and had covered barely three miles when the wagons turned west off the trail and headed into wild country.

He pushed on, his thoughts intent upon the incidents that had occurred back in Coldwater. There was trouble coming, he did not doubt. He could recognize all the signs, as could Sorgan, and was alert to his surroundings. His prime object was to locate Leo Slattery and arrest or kill the man, but he did not mind helping out the sheriff while waiting for Leo to show up.

He had been riding for about two hours when he crossed a skyline and moved down the long decline on the other side. He immediately spotted movement a long way ahead and reined back into cover to observe. A rider was coming along the trail in a tearing hurry, raising dust, pushing the horse along at a killing pace. Loman narrowed his eyes against the glare of the sun and focused on the rider, wondering what had induced the dire effort. No one rode at that speed unless it was a deadly emergency and life was at stake.

The rider came on, using great effort to get the best possible speed out of the lathered horse. Loman shifted his gaze to the rider's back trail, and a sigh escaped him when he saw further movement there as two riders came galloping into view. Gun smoke flared around the head of one of the pursuers, and moments later the report of a shot echoed across the range.

Loman drew his Winchester from its saddle boot

and prepared for action as he awaited developments. The leading rider came on erratically, urging the horse on recklessly. Loman tensed as he recognized the fleeing figure, and then lifted his rifle. It was Kate Hesp heading for town, and she was in a lot of trouble. One of the pursuing riders fired again. Loman saw Kate's horse falter, and then go down with threshing limbs. The girl was thrown from her saddle and landed with a bone jarring thump in the dust.

Cursing under his breath, Loman spurred forward as the girl's two pursuers reached her and sprang from their saddles. He slid his long gun back into its boot and drew his pistol, ready to do battle on the girl's behalf.

FIVE

The sound of Loman's approaching hoof-beats alerted the two men to their danger. Both were bending over Kate and trying to rouse her. They looked up, saw Loman bearing down on them, and reached for their guns. Loman, cocking his pistol the instant he realized they were aware of him, saw that they were intent on shooting at him. He squeezed his trigger. The man on the right pitched over instantly to bury his face in the short grass. The other sprang to his left, dropped to his right knee, and lifted his pistol into the aim.

Loman's gun muzzle followed the man's movements like a hound dog sniffing out a possum. The deadly weapon blasted and the man twisted and fell dead with a slug in the centre of his chest. Loman holstered his pistol and reined in beside the inert Kate. Gun echoes faded slowly into the distance as he checked that both men were dead before he bent over the girl.

Kate was conscious but dazed. There was a smear of blood on her left cheek. Her eyes were flickering, filled with shock, and Loman slid an arm under her slim shoulders and lifted her into a sitting position.

'Are you bad hurt?' he asked softly. 'Try your limbs to see if anything is broken. You took an almighty hard fall.'

She looked up at him, her shock fading slowly from her eyes as she drew a deep breath and spoke in a faltering voice.

'I was being chased by the two gunnies Hub Slattery employs – Bull Craig and Frank Dean. They got between me and the ranch so the only place I could go was Coldwater, but they got in range and shot my horse from under me.'

'I saw the end of the chase,' Loman said.

'Where are those two gunnies?'

'They're close by. They made the mistake of drawing on me when I rode up.'

Kate made an unsuccessful attempt to get to her feet and Loman lifted her easily, holding her steady until she could control her balance. She saw the two men sprawled on the ground and suppressed a shudder.

'Are they dead?' she whispered.

'Of course. They drew together, which didn't give me any time to pick my spots, so I had to shoot to kill. You said they rode for Slattery. Why were they chasing you?'

'I don't know.' Ashen-faced, she shook her head. 'I was taking my morning ride around the ranch and they just showed up. Like I said, they got between me and the house so I ran. I was hoping to get to town before they came up with me.'

Loman sensed that she was not telling the truth. She walked a few tentative steps to check her condition, and winced as her weight shifted to her left leg, but kept moving.

'Nothing seems to be broken,' she commented, turning to face him. 'What happens now? Do you have to tell James that I was involved in this?'

'I don't see how I can keep your name out of it.' Loman frowned. 'Two men are dead, and I've got to have a good reason for killing them.'

'They attacked you without warning. Every man has a right to defend his life.' She spoke eagerly, her eyes wide and serious.

'That ain't likely. Why would they attack me like that? I'm a stranger.'

'You don't have to supply the reason why you were attacked, and they're dead, so they aren't going to tell the truth.'

'Why don't you come clean about what's going on?' he countered. 'I'm on your side. James sent me out here to sort out any problems you and your father might be having. I'm wearing a law badge so I have some protection. I can do anything to set matters right, but only if I know what's going on. Bellamy and Aird attacked you in that alley last night and you wanted to hush that up. It won't do, you know. So what is going on? I've heard that Hub Slattery is mixed up in the rustling, but I can't believe you'd keep quiet about that if it was the only thing wrong. So level with me and I'll know how to handle the situation. I need to know what was happening around here before I rode into town last night, and you seem to be in the middle of it.'

'My father's life is in danger,' she said tensely. 'It's like a nightmare, trying to keep him safe. I don't know which way to turn for the best.'

'You could tell me about it for a start.' Loman's gaze switched from her intent face and he checked their surroundings for movement, turning in a complete circle to look over the undulating range. 'It's obvious Slattery is mixed up in it.' He looked down at the two dead gunmen. 'These two, and Bellamy and Aird last night; they're linked to Hub Slattery. So what is going on?'

'You can ask Slattery himself,' she responded bitterly. 'He's coming over that ridge behind you with a couple of his outfit backing him. I expect he's on his way to town to find out what's happened to his son Wes. They're a close-knit family, and there'll be hell to pay when Hub learns that Wes is in jail.'

Loman swung round, and his right hand dropped to the butt of his holstered pistol when he saw three riders coming along the trail towards them.

'You'd better get out of here pronto,' he said in a clipped tone. 'Mount one of those horses and head for town. Go straight to Sorgan and tell him what's happening. I'll stop these men from following you.'

She began to protest and Loman cut her short, his eyes narrowed as he watched the approach of the three riders.

'Get outa here,' he rapped. 'I don't want you around if shooting starts. You'd be a liability.'

Kate gazed at him in shock, then snatched up the reins of the nearest horse and swung into the saddle.

Loman slapped the horse hard across the rump before she could settle in the saddle, and the animal lunged forward, raising dust as it galloped off along the trail to town. Loman watched her out of sight, then turned to await the arrival of the riders, his face set in harsh lines; deadly gun hand at his side.

As the three riders drew nearer, Loman studied them. The foremost, astride a big grey stallion, was a man in his middle fifties, big, broad-shouldered and rugged of face with a crescent-shaped scar beneath his right eye. He was dressed in good range clothes, and a wide-brimmed grey Stetson shielded his weathered countenance from the harsh rays of the slanting sun. His features were grim, and there was a downturn to his mouth that indicated a bad temperament. He came forward at a mile-eating lope, and Loman knew him by sight because of the family resemblance between him and his son Leo.

The two riders following closely were obviously more than mere cowhands. Both had that alertness which bespoke of hired guns. Their eyes were never still, flickering around to check their surroundings constantly, and their hands were close to the butts of their holstered pistols.

Hub Slattery pulled his mount down to a walk over the last few yards to the spot where Loman was standing with the two dead gunnies at his feet. The HS rancher was staring at the bodies, and horror seeped into his taut features when he recognized them. He reined in and gazed at Loman, his dark eyes filled with shock.

'What in hell happened here?' he demanded,

subjecting Loman to a stare that took in the deputy badge on Loman's chest. 'Who in hell killed them?'

'I did. They drew on me without warning.' Loman spoke quietly. 'I had to kill them.'

One of the other two riders uttered a curse and reached towards his hip, where he had a Remington .44 holstered.

'If you're not faster than either of these two then forget it,' Loman warned.

'Hold it,' Hub Slattery rapped, and the two gunmen froze and sat their saddles with their hard eyes intent on Loman. 'Who was it rode away when we came over the ridge back there? It was the Hesp gal, huh? I might have known she was mixed up in this somewhere. She ain't happy unless she's helling around the county, stirring up the young men and getting them to fight over her. My son Wes is outa his head on account of her. She's got him acting loco, leading him on and then turning him down on account of that fast-draw sheriff in Coldwater. So what happened here to cause my men to try and trade lead with a stranger wearing a deputy badge?'

'I was trying to find that out when you put in an appearance,' Loman said. 'These two were chasing Kate Hesp when I first saw them, and one of them shot the horse from under her. When I came up with them they both lifted their guns, and I was forced to shoot them. So you better tell me what orders you gave them before they left your spread this morning.'

'I didn't tell 'em to shoot at the Hesp gal, if that's what you're thinking.' An animal-like snarl twisted Slattery's thin lips. The strange scar under his right eye was white, untouched by the sun, and Loman wondered what could have made such an injury. 'What kind of a man do you take me for?'

'I don't know a damn thing about anyone in this county,' Loman said tautly. 'I'm in the process of learning. So tell me why two of your gunnies are out hunting your neighbour's daughter.'

'I don't know.' Slattery shook his head. 'But I sure as hell mean to find out. If you hadn't killed them I could have asked. They weren't obeying my orders.'

'What were they supposed to be doing today?' Loman asked.

Slattery shook his head slowly. 'Watching my range, looking for rustlers – anyone out to cause trouble.'

'What about your sons? They're hell-raisers, I've heard.'

'They're young men, entitled to raise a little hell before they settle down to work.'

'Wes is behind bars right now,' Loman broke the news quietly. 'He went too far last night and was arrested.'

'The hell you say!' Slattery dropped his hand to his gun butt. 'What's he done now?'

'He was with three strangers who attacked Kate Hesp, Curly Jackson and Fred Emmet on their way from Coldwater to Double H last night.'

'That's another trick to put blame on my outfit,' Slattery rasped, his dark eyes glittering. 'You can't believe a word said by anyone riding for Double H.'

'I was with them.' Loman shrugged. 'I can believe the evidence of my own eyes, huh? We were ambushed, and when the shooting was over two of the strangers were dead and Wes's horse was down. I rode back to town, told the sheriff, and we picked up Wes shortly afterwards. He said his horse was stolen early that morning and he wasn't riding it when we were attacked. He's been jailed while enquiries are made.'

'He won't be in jail long.' Slattery shook his reins and his horse stepped around the two dead gunnies.

'Hold it,' Loman warned. 'Did you lose cattle and horses two nights ago?'

'I'll talk to the sheriff when I see him.' Slattery kept moving, and Loman palmed his gun and cocked it. Slattery reined up immediately, shock glimmering in his eyes at the evidence of Loman's fast draw. 'Looks like you're mighty keen to start shooting,' he observed. 'Where did the sheriff get you from, and what excuse are you planning to use to gun me down?'

'Answer my question. Did you lose stock two nights ago?'

'Yeah. If Wes said so then we did. He was out on the range all yesterday with some of the crew, looking for sign. A small herd was driven off to the west and they lost tracks on hard ground. Now can I get on to town? I wanta get my boy out of jail.'

'Take your two dead gunnies with you and report to the sheriff,' Loman said.

Hub Slattery looked as if he would refuse, but the unwavering pistol in Loman's hand dissuaded him and he motioned to his two companions, his face expressing fury.

'Load them on that horse and bring them along to town, Taggart,' he said. 'You ride with me, Sam, and we'll get on to Coldwater. I want Wes outa that jail pronto.' He glared at Loman. 'Unless you got other ideas,' he added.

Loman holstered his gun with a deft movement. 'You're free to go where you want,' he replied.

Slattery set spurs to his big horse and the animal lunged forward, hitting full gallop in a few strides. One of the gunmen went with him, and Loman sat his horse while the other dismounted and loaded the dead men on the remaining saddle-horse. Loman remained motionless until Slattery and his companion had disappeared ahead, then turned his horse to follow at a slower pace. He decided to ride back to town, pondering on the situation as far as he knew it and not liking the thoughts that arose in his mind.

Loman noted the hoof prints left by the horse Kate Hesp had taken, and kept an eye on them as he continued. He reined in when he saw where the girl had turned aside from the trail and headed east. If Kate had not ridden to town then he would be wasting his time returning there. He turned aside from the trail and followed the girl's tracks, wishing she had taken him into her confidence. She was certainly in some kind of trouble although she had no intention of seeking help.

She had said her father's life was in danger but had not elaborated on that statement. Loman could only wonder at the problems besetting the girl, and pushed his horse into a faster gait. He soon discovered that Kate had turned left and headed back north, regaining the trail to Double H some three miles beyond the spot where the shooting had occurred. He settled himself to covering ground, guided only by the girl's tracks on the trail.

Two hours of steady riding brought him in sight of a large ranch, and he looked around speculatively as he approached it. An imposing house stood on a knoll overlooking a wide creek. There was a big barn and numerous smaller buildings off to the left, with two corrals further to the left. The place looked to be in a state of good repair.

Loman rode through a tall gateway and headed for the house, where he could see a horse standing at a hitch rail in front of the porch. He recognized the animal as the one Kate had ridden, and was determined to get an explanation from her. He could not understand why she was refusing all help.

Kate came out to the porch as Loman dismounted, and there was defiance in her expression as he confronted her.

'I didn't hear any shooting when I left you,' she said. 'I was hoping you'd kill Hub Slattery.'

'Why didn't you ride into town?' he countered. 'You should have reported what happened on the trail.'

'I needed to get back here. James wouldn't do anything to help me. He won't do anything if his precious law hasn't been broken.'

'That's an odd thing to say about the man you're intending to marry. From what I know of James, he would move heaven and earth to save you from trouble.'

'Why didn't you ride into town?' she demanded.

'I was given the chore of riding out here to keep an eye on you. When I saw your tracks turning off it would have been a waste of time going on while you rode in the opposite direction.'

'You'd better come into the house now you're here.' Her tone eased but she spoke grudgingly. 'I don't know what you think you can do to help, but it would take an army to remove the threat against my father.'

'Tell me about it and I'll make up my own mind about what to do. I'm not going away, so you'd better accept the situation and try to make my job easier.'

She led the way into the house. Loman removed his hat as they passed through a large, square living-room to enter a kitchen.

'I was about to make coffee,' Kate said. 'Would you like some?'

Loman nodded, and sat down at a long table. He watched her making coffee. When it was ready she came to the table, placed a big cup before him, then sat down opposite. He remained silent, and she was induced to fill the void.

'We've been getting trouble for weeks now,' she said slowly, her eyes expressing uncertainty. 'There's always been trouble as long as I can remember, and I reckon Hub Slattery is to blame. He and my father were in the army together during the war, and there was some bad trouble between them in those days which has never been settled. They had been close friends up until the war – I never found out what caused the trouble between them – but they never spoke after they came home.'

She lapsed into silence and Loman watched her expression as she sat gazing at her coffee. He could feel a strand of some indefinable emotion unwinding in his mind, and tried to block it because he had no wish to become interested in her personally. He stifled his impatience.

'So what makes you think your father's life is in danger?' he asked.

'Father and I were coming back from town about six weeks ago when a shot was fired at him from cover. He wasn't hit. I think it was only a warning. Dad hasn't left the ranch since, and he's taken on several gunhands. I've tried to talk to him about it but he's kept his mouth shut, and I know he's keeping something from me. There have been three instances of cattle-stealing, small stuff each time, but amounting to a big loss when added together. Again, Dad didn't do anything about it. He seems to be content just to keep the troublemakers away from the house.'

'Why haven't you told James about this? He'd put a stop to whatever is going on.'

'I've tried to tell him but he won't listen. He thinks the Slatterys are behind it, and says he can't do a thing to help until the law has been broken and he has proof of wrong-doing.'

'Well, I'm here now, and you'll be better off doing like I say. In future, don't go riding alone. Stay close to the ranch until I can look around and find out what's going on. I'll shadow you over the next few days and watch for another attempt to take you.'

'Set me up as a target, you mean,' she countered. 'And what happens if you make a hash of it if I am attacked again? I shall be probably be killed.'

He saw the bruise on her face which she had collected when her horse was shot from under her, and a chill touched him as he considered.

'If I can think of a better way to handle this deal then I'll use it. If I'm on hand when another try for you is made, I'll be in a position to do something about it.'

'Considering the way this business is affecting my father, I have no option but to go along with you,' she replied, sighing heavily. 'OK. I'll do what I can to help.'

'Good. Accept that I'm a friend whose only wish is to help, and we will soon settle this,' he rejoined.

'You'd better sleep in the house.' She stood up abruptly and turned away. He watched her cross to the door, where she paused and looked back at him. 'I'll get a room ready for you, and while I'm doing that you can talk to my father. He might have objections to a deputy staying in the house. I'll tell him you're here. Drink your coffee and I'll come for you if Dad wants to see you.'

She departed, and Loman frowned as he drank the coffee, his forehead creased while he considered her attitude. She seemed to have an attitude about Sorgan which was at odds with her intended marriage to him. He surmised that much was going on behind the scenes that had not been communicated to him, and wondered just what kind of a situation he was encountering.

Kate returned shortly, and her manner had eased somewhat. She actually smiled as she paused in the doorway.

'Dad is in his office and he'll see you now. I'll show you the way. You can tell him the truth about why you are here. He may disagree with you and want you to leave, but tell him you are under orders from James and he'll accept the inevitable.'

Loman nodded and arose from the table. He followed her into the hall and she showed him into a room on the left, pausing at the door, and then closing it after he had entered. He heard her footsteps moving away along the hall as he glanced around the room before looking at the big man seated behind a large, leather-topped desk in front of a tall window that gave an extensive view of the yard. Loman noticed that the desk was completely bare, uncluttered, with no evidence of paperwork.

Henry Hesp was approaching sixty, and his wrinkled face was wearing a frown that spoke of his inner uneasiness. His large features were dark, weather-beaten, his cheeks thin, his lips permanently set in an uncompromising line. He was big-boned, his frame covered with lean flesh that spoke of long years of hard living. His brown eyes were wary as he got to his feet and thrust a large brown hand across the desk. Loman gripped it briefly.

'Howdy, son,' Hesp said. 'Glad to know you. You're Ward Loman, huh? Well, I'm glad to know any man who is a friend of James Sorgan. He's a fine sheriff. What's doing in town these days? Must be all of six weeks since I was last over that way.'

'I can understand that,' Loman said quietly. 'I heard that you were shot at from cover the last time you rode back from town.'

Hesp sank back into his seat and motioned Loman to a chair adjacent to the desk, his jaw muscles tightening into bulging lines as he clenched his teeth, and a sigh escaped him.

'Yeah.' He nodded. 'We got all kinds of trouble coming to this range.'

'I figure you know who shot at you. Is that a fact?' Loman kept his tone easy, and a faint smile showed on his lips as Hesp gazed at him in shock.

'Hell, I'd have done something about that ambusher if I had any idea who he was. What makes you think I should know him?'

'He fired a shot that missed, and rode away without trying to nail you.'

'He was scared of getting caught, I should think.'

'And you stayed close to the ranch after it happened, while any man would have moved heaven and earth to get the ambusher. You're running scared is my guess, and that is at odds with the kind of man I think you are. I've been sent here by Sorgan to get you through your troubles, and I sure hope you're gonna help me all you can.'

'I'm afraid you've had your ride out from town for nothing. There's nothing going on around here that my outfit can't handle. I appreciate Sorgan's concern for my welfare, and while I admire him greatly for the way he's taming the county, I don't like his cold-blooded ways. I'm sure you'll understand why I'm turning down any help he offers.'

'So you'd like me to leave, despite the fact that your daughter is caught up in this affair and, while you're skulking here on your ranch, she is in danger of being killed by the hardcases who have moved in on the range.'

Hesp gazed at Loman with shock seeping into his eyes. He shook his head in denial of Loman's words, and beads of sweat broke out on his forehead as his shoulders slumped. The next instant he gasped and clutched at his chest, then fell forward on the desk and lapsed into unconsciousness before Loman could react.

SIX

Loman moved around the desk and bent over Hesp to take hold of the rancher's right wrist and check the pulse, which was rapid. Hesp was breathing heavily, irregularly. Loman ran to the door and went into the hall. He called for Kate, his harsh voice echoing in the deep silence enveloping the house. She emerged from a room further along the hall and came running to his side.

'Your father has collapsed,' he said, and saw her expression change.

She pushed by him and ran into the room to go to her father's side. Hesp was regaining his senses, making an ineffectual effort to sit up straight. His face was ashen, his eyes flickering, and Kate put an arm around his shoulders.

'Don't try to move, Dad,' she said sharply. 'I'll get your medicine, and then have a couple of the men take you up to your bed.'

'I'll be all right,' Hesp responded. 'Why didn't you tell me you've had some trouble, Kate?'

'I didn't want to worry you.' She glanced at Loman

with anger in her dark gaze. 'Just stay quiet while I get that physic Doc Pearson gave you.'

She hurried from the room. Loman stood motionless. Hesp pushed himself into a sitting position and held himself upright by pressing his palms against the top of the desk. His face was regaining some of its colour, but his eyes were filled with shock as he looked up at Loman.

'I'm glad you're here, son,' he mumbled. 'Take no notice of me. You keep your attention fixed on Kate – keep her safe from the wolves that are gathering.'

'Perhaps we can talk when you're feeling better,' Loman suggested. 'I need to know some of the background to your problems if I'm to help.'

'I guess you're right. We'll get together later.'

Kate returned, carrying a small bottle and a spoon. She administered a spoonful of the medicine, and Hesp leaned back in his seat and closed his eyes. His forehead was beaded with sweat, and Kate patted it dry with a handkerchief. Loman heard footsteps in the hall, and then two men appeared in the doorway.

'Come in, Bill,' Kate said urgently. 'Dad is having an attack. Carry him up to his bedroom and undress him, please.' Her eyes slid to Loman's face as the two men entered the room. 'This is Bill McKay, the ranch foreman, and our cook, Cartwheel Johnson,' she introduced.

McKay was around forty years old, large, rawboned, over six feet in height, and looking tough enough to push over a barn. He glanced at Loman, his dark gaze resting for a moment on the law star on Loman's chest. His companion, Cartwheel Johnson, was small, wiry, pushing sixty at least, with a wrinkled face that carried a vinegary scowl. Both men went around the desk and, despite Hesp's protests, laid gentle hands on him and lifted him out of his seat.

'There ain't no need for that kind of talk, Cap'n,' McKay said easily in a booming voice that seemed to start from his boots, and Hesp stopped his cursing. 'Miss Kate is right and you know it. Let's get you to your bed, this time without any fuss. I heard what the doc said when he was here last week, so it ain't no good you pulling against the reins. Just rest up and let us get this done easy.'

They carried Hesp out of the room and Kate followed closely. Loman walked into the hall and stood at the foot of the stairs. McKay's heavy voice sounded all over the house, soothing and sometimes remonstrating against Hesp's protests. Moments later, McKay and Johnson descended the stairs. Johnson glanced at Loman and departed without a word. McKay would have done the same but Loman stepped in front of the big foreman.

'I'd like to talk to you, Bill,' Loman said.

'Come outside,' the foreman responded.

Loman followed the man out of the house and they stood on the porch, gazing across the wide yard. The sun was in its noon position. Short shadows lay on the spread, and heat packed in around them, fierce as the inside of an oven. The breeze was hot as a lizard's tongue, and Loman felt sweat breaking out on his forehead.

'I ain't seen you around before,' McKay said. 'How long you been in the county?'

'A couple of days, which ain't long enough to learn what's going on. What is the trouble blowing up around this spread?'

McKay looked into Loman's face, his expression placid. He shook his head.

'It ain't for me to talk about family business. You'll have to ask the Cap'n about things like that.'

'He ain't in a position to talk at the moment, and from what I've seen, the sooner I get a slant on the trouble the easier it will be for Kate.'

'What do you mean? Have they tried to get to her?' McKay cursed softly. 'I thought Curly Jackson looked sheepish when they got back from town last night. If he ain't been doing his job right I'll make him wish he'd never been born.'

Loman explained the incidents that had taken place in Coldwater the night before, and ended with a graphic account of Kate's horse being shot from under her earlier that morning. He saw McKay's face turn pale under its tan, and the foreman's brown eyes glinted as he clenched his big hands.

'Jeez!' he exclaimed. 'I've been warning Kate to stay close to home, and the Cap'n don't ever take notice of advice from anyone. I set Jackson and Emmet as bodyguards to Kate, against her wishes, I might add, but they'd sooner obey her orders than mine, and they ain't no great shakes as bodyguards. I'm tempted to fire that pair of no-goods.'

'You called Hesp "Captain",' Loman observed. 'Were you in the war with him?'

'Sure. I was his sergeant. We had some tough times together.'

'Who didn't?' Loman made an effort to keep his thoughts away from his own war service. 'I've been sent here by the sheriff to make sure nothing bad happens to Kate. She isn't keen on the idea but I've got a job to do and no one and nothing is going to stop me. If you know anything about what's going on then I'd like to hear it'

'I won't open my mouth 'less Miss Kate says I can.' McKay shook his head and his right hand rested on the pistol holstered on his hip. 'You said Wes Slattery was mixed up in that attack last night?'

'That's right, and I killed two HS gunnies this morning – Dean and Craig.'

A trace of respect showed momentarily in McKay's gaze, then it was gone. He nodded slowly, catching his lower lip between his teeth as he wrestled with his sense of duty.

'That's more than Sorgan has done in his time here,' McKay mused. 'I don't know which side of the fence the sheriff is on. He talks a lot about proof, but anyone with half an eye can see the Slatterys are pushing for trouble. It's about time we went on the war path to defend this spread. If we leave it too late, then one fine morning the Slatterys will be swarming all over us.'

'What happened during the war to set Hesp and Slattery against each other?'

'What do you know about that?' McKay grimaced and his eyes narrowed. 'No one is supposed to know about it. Who in heck has been running off at the lip to you? I'll drag his tongue out by its root if I lay hands on him.'

'I don't know about it. That's why I'm asking. Kate told me her father and Slattery were friends before the war, but when they came home afterwards they never spoke to each other again. It's got to be mighty serious to ruin a friendship, and this trouble could have its roots in that.'

McKay shook his head. 'Things happen during war-time that don't compare with anything before or after. I'm under oath not to talk about it, so my lips are clamped tight, and wild horses couldn't drag them open.'

'Even if something bad may happen to Kate if you don't speak up?'

'I'll have to take that chance. I'm watching the gal pretty close myself.'

'But twice in the last twenty-four hours she was at risk, and you were nowhere around to give help when she needed it. I saved her both times. I've been sent here to watch out for her, so you'd better tell me anything that could help do my job.'

'I'm sure glad you showed up when you did, I got to admit. I'll tell you anything I know about the general situation on the range, but that war thing is not to be mentioned.'

'Do you have proof that the Slatterys are back of the local rustling?' Loman persisted.

'There's no proof, because if there was then the Slatterys would be swinging in the breeze now. I've heard rumours, and I know Wes and Charlie Slattery as a couple of hell-raisers, but that don't make them cattle-thieves.'

'But now you know that two HS gunnies shot

Kate's horse from under her this morning, what are you gonna do about it?'

'I know what I'd like to do but I ain't the boss of this outfit. I take orders the same as everybody else. You saw for yourself that the Cap'n ain't a well man. I can't bully him into anything. I have to walk soft around him.'

Loman heaved a sigh and gave up. He went back into the house and found Kate in the kitchen, preparing a meal. She glanced sideways at him and he could tell by her expression that she was badly worried about her father. He sat down at the table, hoping her fears would loosen her tongue. When she did not speak he arose and went to her side.

'Your father knew the man who shot at him,' he rasped. 'It was a shot that was meant as a warning. You both knew it wasn't meant to kill. I figure that someone was putting pressure on your dad – wanted him to know that he or you could be killed at any time. Am I right?'

'I don't know anything about that.' Kate shook her head. 'It sounds unlikely. What could anyone want from us that would call for such an action?

'I sure wish I knew.' Loman was aware that he would get nothing from her and tried another tack. 'Do you want me to ride back to town and tell James you don't want my help?' he asked.

She was startled by his change of attack and paused in what she was doing, her hands clenching as she considered. Then she continued working.

'You must think I am very ungrateful,' she ventured.

'What I think doesn't come into it. There's only one thought in my mind, if you must know. I want to see that nothing bad happens to you, and you can make that an easy chore by giving me all the information you have, or you can make it an impossible job by clamming up. If you stay dumb then I'll probably see you lying dead somewhere soon, because men like those two I killed this morning will certainly get to you when I'm not around.'

He fell silent to give her an opportunity to think over his stark words. They seemed to have the desired effect because she drew a deep breath and then shuddered. A shadow crossed her pale face as she released her pent-up breath in a long sigh and hope showed momentarily in her eyes. She sighed again.

'Where would I start to unravel such a train of incidents?' She grimaced. 'I think it's too late to stop the situation that is unfolding.'

'The further it goes the harder it will get,' he commented, and saw her nod. 'Why don't you let me ask the questions, and you just fill in the answers? That way I can get to the bottom of it. Why did you meet Aird and Bellamy in that alley in town?'

'I didn't meet them in the alley. I was on the sidewalk and they came up behind me. Aird said he wanted me to carry a message to my father. I know Aird as a cattle-buyer. He came out here a couple of times last year, and although I don't know the actual details, he tried to get cattle from Dad without paying for them – a case of pure blackmail. Father ran him off the place, and threatened to shoot him if he ever returned. That's why I refused to carry a message, and Aird got nasty. He pushed me into the alley, and I became afraid for my life. I screamed when he laid hands on me, and that's when you appeared.'

'So what has your dad done in the past that Aird could use to blackmail him?'

'Nothing! Dad is an honest man. You can ask anyone in the county and you'll get the same answer.'

'Then something must have happened in the war. There was something, because it turned your father against Hub Slattery.'

'I wouldn't know about that.'

Loman waited for her to continue but she remained silent. Impatience crept into his mind and he sighed as he smothered it and searched for another angle to pursue.

'What shall I tell James about all this?' he asked. 'You'd rather run the risk of being killed than give me the situation. It must be pretty bad if you are prepared to die rather than talk. I can't think of anything that would make me clam up, if death was the alternative. But, considering your attitude, I think I'm wasting my time. James will have to take over. He should be able to deal with you.'

'Don't go.' She looked into his eyes and he could see turmoil in her gaze. 'Just wait a bit longer. A couple of days can't hurt. James told you to stick around and watch points, so why don't you do that? Dad is waiting for a visitor to arrive shortly and when he shows up this business might simmer down again.'

'You're making the situation sound even more

suspicious,' Loman mused, 'but I'll go along with it. I'll take a look around the spread now, if you don't mind.'

'Sure. I'll call you when the noon meal is ready.'

Loman left the house and took his horse across to the nearer of the corrals. After caring for the animal he turned to see Bill McKay standing in the doorway of the barn watching him. McKay motioned for Loman to join him, and moved back into the shadows of the barn as Loman approached.

Impatience was growing in Loman's mind. He was mentally exhausted by the questions he had asked in vain, and was on the point of giving up and riding back to talk over the situation with Sorgan. He paused in the doorway of the barn and squinted against the gloom pervading the place. There was a back door, which stood open, and he saw McKay bending over the figure of a man sprawled inertly in the dust. Frowning, he went to the foreman's side, and a stab of horror struck through him when he found himself looking down into Al Donovan's pale face. The deputy was unconscious.

'Where did he come from?' Loman demanded.

'I don't know. I came in here to check around and found him lying just outside. His horse is out there. He must have slipped out of the saddle when it stopped there, and crawled inside. He's been shot in the back, low down on the right just under the bottom rib. He's still alive, but he sure is in a bad way. I'm wondering what in hell he was doing out here, and what trouble he found.'

'Sorgan sent him out to check on a couple of

wagons heading out of town last night – half a dozen tough riders and a deputy US marshal riding under the command of a Major Bracknell. One of those men shot Joel Bender in town for just nosing around the wagons. He's in jail, and the sheriff wants to know what the outfit is up to.'

While he spoke, Loman dropped to one knee beside Donovan and eased him into a sitting position. The back of the deputy's shirt was soaked with blood. He looked up at McKay, and found the ramrod gazing intently at him, shock on his face.

'What's wrong?' Loman demanded. 'Don't tell me you can't stand the sight of blood?'

'It was what you said. You mentioned Major Bracknell. Was he in town?'

'Yeah.' Loman nodded. 'He's got the coldest blue eyes I ever saw. Do you know him?'

'I'll say I do.' A trace of bitterness touched McKay's deep voice. 'So he's finally caught up with us. He's a head-hunter for the Union army. I met him just after the war finished, when the bluecoats were hunting a squad of confederate raiders – something about a big consignment of Union gold that had gone missing just before the cease-fire. Cap'n Hesp led a patrol to grab a consignment of Union gold, but didn't get it. I missed that patrol so I don't know what really happened. But I do know Bracknell ain't a man to be trifled with. He had some Confederates shot out of hand, and got away with it. He's hell on wheels, and then some. I got no idea what he's doing around here, the war being over several years now.'

'You'd better send a man into town to fetch the doc,' Loman said, 'and tell him to report this to Sorgan.'

'What are you going to do?' McKay asked.

'Track Donovan's horse to check on where he came from and what happened.'

'I think Donovan will be dead before the doc gets here.' McKay sighed heavily. 'If you see the Cap'n, don't mention Bracknell. The shock might kill him.'

'Why? Is that missing gold the reason why there's trouble here? Is it what caused the rift between Slattery and your boss?'

McKay turned away. 'I'd better get someone on his way to town,' he said.

Loman let him go and went out the back door. A horse was standing with trailing reins, head down as if it had travelled fast for a long period. Loman grasped the reins and led the animal into the barn. He took it through to the water-trough outside the front door and allowed it to drink, then tethered it to a post just inside the barn. He went back to Donovan, saw the deputy's eyes flickering, and dropped to one knee beside him.

'Donovan, can you hear me?' he demanded.

The deputy's eyes flickered opened. They were filled with shock, but cleared slowly. Donovan gazed up at him. Blood was trickling from a corner of his mouth. He grinned weakly.

'Howdy, Loman. What are you doing here? This is Double H, huh?'

'Sure. What happened to you?'

'I got a mite careless, I reckon. Followed that

Bracknell outfit out to Poison Creek. Rode in too close. One of the outfit was riding point, and circled around the wagons to check for sign that they were being followed. He picked up my tracks, and shot me in the back when I tried to make a run for it.'

'Shot you without warning?' Loman frowned as he considered. 'What in hell is that bunch up to? They're far too free with their shooting for my liking.'

'They sure ain't friendly. You got to get word to Sorgan, and I need the doc to check me over.'

'It's being arranged.' Loman got to his feet when he saw that Donovan had slipped back into unconsciousness. He went outside to examine the hoof prints left by the deputy's horse.

McKay returned with two men and Donovan was lifted and carried to the house. Loman went for his horse, and he was ready to ride by the time McKay emerged from the house.

'Where's Poison Creek?' Loman asked.

McKay frowned. 'It's to the west of here, lying between HS and Double H; fenced off because it's dangerous to stock. It lies in broken ground. There's something wrong with the water.'

'That's where Major Bracknell and his outfit are. I'll ride in that direction to take a look around.'

'Watch out for Bracknell.' McKay spoke raggedly. 'He's hell on the hoof. I heard a lot of talk about him after the war. He took a lot of good Confederates and hanged 'em high in the name of justice, but was using his position to get at money said to be stolen from the blue-bellies, and it was said that a lot of what he recovered didn't get back to where it rightfully belonged.'

'So why is he in this county?' Loman mused. 'He must be looking for men who live around here.'

'He's got a nose like a hound dog.' McKay shook his head. 'I guess this trouble has to come to a head, and it's been a long time festering. I would have settled for a good, old-fashioned case of rustling. We could have hung the rustlers and it would be finished, but this business is out of hand, and the wrong folks could suffer.'

'You're talking in riddles,' Loman said. 'Is there anything I ought to know before I ride? Tell me about the missing gold and why Bracknell is interested in men living around here.'

'Like I said, if you want to know about that then you better ask the Cap'n.' There was a note of finality in McKay's voice, and Loman shook his head and departed. He mounted and rode through the barn to pick up Donovan's tracks, then rode out at a fast clip, trying to control his impatience.

If he could not learn about the trouble building up by asking questions then he would have to do it the hard way and face the men who had some of the answers.

SEVEN

Loman rode steadily, back-tracking the prints left by Donovan's horse. He felt that he was getting to the heart of the trouble besetting this range, and gave his thoughts free rein as he headed west. He had served in the Union Army during the war, but felt no sympathy for those men who had used the conflict in order to grab illegal spoils for themselves. Five years had passed since General Lee surrendered, and there was still serious ill-feeling in the South at how the North was handling its post-war policies.

He kept a strict watch on his surroundings. Donovan had been attacked without warning by one of Major Bracknell's party, and Joel Bender had been slain in Coldwater by another of the same group. Bracknell was obviously a fanatic who pursued his duty without due regard to the law or the guilt or innocence of those he hunted. That he was in Tate County could be the reason for the trouble brewing, and Loman was intrigued by the apparent situation. It seemed that a web of conspiracy had been woven around the county and was being spun tighter and tighter.

His main interest was the whereabouts of Leo Slattery, but he was being drawn irrevocably into Kate Hesp's problems, and felt justified in using his talents and skill to aid the local law while awaiting Leo's arrival.

The tracks he followed were plain, and he made good time. An hour after leaving Double H he reached a spot where a second set of hoof prints, following Donovan's tracks from the opposite direction, had halted and turned back the way they had come. He studied them at length and, when he continued, was doubly alert, certain that the new prints had been made by the man who had shot Donovan.

Loman moved cautiously up inclines and checked the way ahead by exposing no more than his eyes over the ridges he encountered. Peering across a ridge some time later, he saw Poison Creek in the distance, glinting dully under the dark scum that marred its surface. Bracknell's two wagons were standing beside the stretch of water in the scant shade of stunted trees; teams unhitched and grazing on short grass. Figures were moving around the camp, and Loman saw a guard watching the approaches.

He eased back off the ridge and rode back the way he had come until he was well clear, then travelled east for a mile before turning north-west, intent upon circling Bracknell's camp and approaching from the far side. If Bracknell was using his official status to further illicit business, it would explain the callousness with which his security was being maintained. Loman assumed that Bracknell was playing for big stakes if he was prepared to murder indiscriminately.

The sudden rapid beat of hoofs in his rear alerted Loman and he turned his horse into a clump of bushes. He slid from the saddle, drew his pistol and eased forward to observe. A sigh escaped him when he recognized Kate Hesp trailing him almost at a gallop. He holstered his pistol and stepped out into the open. The girl spotted him and changed direction slightly, raised dust towards him, and then pulled her horse to a slithering halt and sat gazing down at him.

'Are you trying to set fire to the range?' Loman demanded. 'And you don't learn by your experiences, riding out alone after what happened this morning.'

'I wanted to stop you before you tangled with Bracknell,' Kate gasped. 'Bill McKay told me what he said to you about the stolen gold shipment, and I don't want you taking action on the wrong information. You think my father or Hub Slattery stole that gold, don't you?'

'I don't think anything at all,' he responded, 'and I never jump to conclusions. I have suspicions, yes, but I'd never act on them. Donovan told me he was shot by one of Bracknell's men, so I'm here to find out what is going on. As to the stolen gold shipment, that's got nothing to do with me so I'll leave it to others to deal with.' He paused, and then said:

'Don't tell me you've had a sudden change of heart.'

Kate slipped out of her saddle and led her horse into the bushes. Loman looked around and saw a horseman descending a slope to their left and then ride steadily in the direction of Double H. Fortunately the man was too far to the right to spot their tracks, but if he continued in the same direction for more than a couple of miles he would be bound to cross Loman's original tracks.

They watched the man until he was out of sight, and then Loman led his horse out of the bushes.

'We'd better get out of here,' he said. 'Let's ride east a couple of miles before swinging south. That will take us away from Bracknell's bunch, and you can tell me what you know about the trouble as we ride back to Double H. After that I'll wanta know why you've disobeyed my orders. I told you never to ride out alone after the trouble you had earlier.'

'It was an emergency,' she said defensively as they rode, 'and things are not as you think.'

'You'll have to tell me what it is you think I'm thinking,' he responded, 'because I don't know what to think.'

'You believe my father and Hub Slattery stole that gold, then fell out over it and are now enemies.'

'That had crossed my mind.' Loman smiled. 'It's the obvious angle, but I like to keep a clear mind, so tell me now what really happened.'

'That's the trouble. I don't know. My father thinks Slattery stole it and, obviously, Slattery thinks my father was responsible.'

'Why don't you start at the beginning? The more

you say the less I'm sure of.'

'It happened during the last weeks of the war. The Confederates learned of a large gold shipment being transported behind Union lines. My father was sent in command of a patrol to seize the shipment, and Hub Slattery was detailed to duplicate the patrol to ensure its success. My father didn't know of Slattery's patrol, and Slattery reached their destination first and carried out the raid. My father arrived after Slattery's patrol had broken off the action and headed back across the Union line.'

Kate paused and moistened her lips, her eyes filled with worry.

'Dad confronted Slattery, who said all he found were boxes filled with sand and rocks. Someone had beaten them to the gold. Slattery accused my father of being responsible, and Dad naturally thought Slattery was guilty. There was an investigation when they returned to their headquarters but it was inconclusive. The war was ending and Dad was discharged under a cloud, as was Slattery. They've been suspicious of each other ever since, each convinced that the other had stolen a march and got away with the gold.'

'It should have been easy to get at the truth.' Loman glanced around to check that they were not being observed. 'The Union would have hounded your father and Slattery if they suspected either of them was guilty of lifting the consignment. And with Bracknell in the county and nosing around, it looks like he knows something about what really happened to the gold. McKay said he knew something of

Bracknell's activities during the war, and they weren't good. The major, it seems, has a bad record.'

'We'll talk to Bill when we get back to the ranch,' Kate promised. 'I realize now that I've had the wrong attitude about this whole mess. I've been scared to chase after the truth in case it came out that Dad did have a hand in something dishonest. I don't believe he did, but strange things happen where gold is involved.'

'What was the value of the missing consignment?' Loman glanced over his left shoulder to check their back trail. He was concerned about the rider they had seen and his alertness was sending repeated warnings through his mind.

'Two hundred thousand US dollars.' Kate sighed. 'A lot of men would murder for much less than that.'

'And if your father was not responsible for it going missing then you think Hub Slattery took it.'

'That's about the weight of it.' She nodded.

'How many men rode with your father on the raid?'

'Ten, and the same number accompanied Slattery.'

'So if either your father or Slattery stole the gold it would have involved a squad of cavalry. I think one of them at least would have talked about the theft, don't you? Or was the gold shared out among them? Two hundred thousand dollars in gold makes a heavy load to transport, or was it hidden someplace close to where it was stolen and collected after hostilities ceased? Has any gold turned up around here since, or is it still hidden, waiting to be shared out?'

'I haven't heard of anyone suddenly becoming rich, but two hundred thousand dollars in gold works out to a lot of money per man if were to be shared between either Dad's or Slattery's patrol.' Kate sighed. 'This has been like a nightmare ever since I first heard of it. I don't know if Dad is guilty or not and, now Major Bracknell has showed up, anything could happen. What can we do about it, Ward?'

'I can check it out,' he responded, 'if I get the time to do it. But Donovan being shot by Bracknell's outfit suggests that the major is pushing for a result. We need to talk to your father and Slattery to get at the truth of what happened on that raid. If we can clear either or both of them then the rest should be a matter of simple investigation. Do you know if your dad or Hub Slattery knew Bracknell before the war?'

'I don't know.' Kate shook her head. 'I hope you're right about getting to the truth quickly. I don't think I can take much more of this uncertainty, and Dad has made himself ill worrying about it. I'm sure Slattery is the guilty man. He got to the gold shipment first. The mystery had evolved by the time Dad reached it.'

'Don't jump to conclusions,' Loman warned. 'Have you thought about this from Slattery's angle?'

'How do you mean?'

'Suppose Slattery is guilty. What did he do with the gold? His patrol didn't have it with them when your father arrived so it must have been hidden nearby, because he didn't take it when he rode back to Confederate lines with your father. Has it been recovered since by the thieves? It's obvious that if

Bracknell stole it he wouldn't be here now, nosing around. He's obviously still looking for it.'

Kate nodded. She seemed relieved now for having taken Loman into her confidence. He looked around, checking for movement in their surroundings, and at that moment a rifle cracked in the distance. Loman's head jerked round, looking for tell-tale gun smoke. His horse stopped suddenly, as if it had run into the side of a barn. Loman felt the animal shudder, and then it went down heavily. He kicked his feet clear of the stirrups, threw himself sideways and, as he hit the ground hard on his left shoulder, his head struck a large rock.

Loman felt no pain. Blackness swooped in upon him like an attacking eagle and he lost consciousness. . . .

Later, his returning senses brought him back to a reality that was laced with pain. He opened his eyes to find the sun far over to the west and night preparing to steal in across the range, distributing grey shadows in all the low places. He lifted his hand to his aching head, struggling to recall what had happened. There was dried blood on his left temple. He tried to ease himself into a sitting position, but was unable to move. He slumped and closed his eyes, struggling against throbbing pain.

His thoughts became animated and he recalled the shot – his horse falling. Then he thought of Kate Hesp, and wondered why she had not come to his aid. He made a superhuman effort to lift his head, and blinked rapidly as he looked around. He saw nothing but his dead horse stretched out only feet away. He rolled on to his right side and thrust an elbow against the ground to lever himself up. His head protested against the movement but he persisted, and eventually managed to sit up. A dull throbbing in his head gave him trouble and his senses swam, then settled down. He pushed himself to his feet.

Loman stood beside his horse and looked around. He saw tracks where Kate's horse had run off to the west at a fast pace. The shot, he recalled, had come from straight ahead, and he guessed that the rider they had seen a short time before the ambush had been alerted by the sight of his earlier tracks. He calculated that he had been lying unconscious for two hours at least, and looked more closely at the tracks Kate had left. She had moved out fast with, he suspected, the ambusher pursuing her.

He stripped his saddle-bags from the horse and drew his rifle from its boot. He threw the bags across his left shoulder and set off, following the girl's tracks. The rays of the sun struck him in the eyes and he moved unsteadily, aware that there was nothing he could do but follow the tracks and hope that Kate had escaped.

In the space of a short distance Loman realized that he was in dire straits. Walking in riding-boots was not a good idea. The ground was much rougher on foot than it had seemed from the back of a horse. He dropped to his knees more than once, aware that the blow to his head when he fell had weakened him considerably. His thoughts rambled, his coolness of mind and intelligence strangely unbalanced. He reached a spot where the tracks of a second horse joined those left by Kate's animal, and guessed the girl had fallen into the wrong hands again. He was still walking when night fell and he could no longer see the tracks Kate had left. He spotted the gleam of a camp-fire ahead, showing dimly through the brush, and his optimism was fired by the thought that help could be at hand.

He went on, his steps lagging, but his mind was more finely attuned now, and the pain of his head wound had eased considerably. The moon was showing faintly, half-hidden by a distant peak, and pale silvery lunar light diluted the darkness but made it deceptive. Dark shadows lay everywhere, and Loman feared that he was stumbling into Bracknell's camp, for if he was then all he could expect was a lethal reception.

He dropped to his knees on the outskirts of the camp and soon realized that it belonged to Bracknell. The two wagons were still in the place where he had seen them earlier, and he could hear the sound of horses grazing in the shadows nearby. The camp-fire was low, the camp silent, and Loman, flat on his belly, looked around for signs of occupation. There were several bedrolls around the fire, but they seemed empty, and he frowned as he tried to size up the situation.

He was certain there would be a guard on watch, and his spine tingled in anticipation as he looked for the man's position, his head turning very slowly as his eyes tried to pierce the surrounding shadows. The silence was intense, the stillness supreme.

Somewhere a horse coughed harshly, invisible in the impenetrable shadows.

Loman did not move, and almost immediately his patience paid off. His attention was attracted by a slight movement in the shadows to his right, and then a figure on foot moved slowly into the camp, carrying a rifle and looking around with all the assurance and alertness of a military guard.

The man paused beside one of the wagons and bent to examine someone lying in blankets in the darker shadows surrounding the vehicle. The low murmur of voices sounded, and Loman picked up a woman's tone, sharp and complaining, and sensed that he had discovered Kate Hesp's whereabouts. The guard laughed in a grating tone and moved away to continue his round of the camp.

Where were the rest of Bracknell's crew? The thought instilled caution in Loman as he circled to the right while the guard moved off to the left. He approached a picket line and saw only the wagon teams standing in a line in the prescribed military fashion. There were no saddle-horses, and he suspected that Bracknell was absent from the camp on some unlawful chore.

He went on, emboldened by his discovery. It looked as if the odds of the opposition were even. Only the guard was present, and he crawled through the shadows towards the wagon where the woman was lying. He moved carefully, aware that he could be wrong about the woman's identity. If Kate was here he would have no trouble, but if another woman occupied those blankets there would be hell to pay.

Loman crawled into the shadows around the rear of the wagon and paused, his gaze narrowed to pierce the shadows. He saw the indistinct shape of a blanket roll on the ground beside a big back wheel and placed his saddle-bags close to hand and laid his rifle beside them. There was a rustling sound as the occupant of the blankets moved restlessly, and Loman slid forward and hurled himself upon the spot. His right hand went out to clamp tightly over the mouth of the sleeper, and he knew by the instant reaction that he had located a woman.

'Don't cry out,' he hissed. 'I'm Loman. Give me your name.'

He eased the pressure of his hand on her mouth.

'Kate Hesp,' she replied in a muffled tone. 'I've been waiting for you. What took you so long?'

'I was asleep for a couple of hours. What happened to you?' Loman's gaze searched the camp for signs of the guard.

'The ambusher caught up with me. I was afraid you were dead. Are you all right?'

'I am now,' he replied.

'Then untie me and get me out of here,' she responded. 'Major Bracknell and his men rode out just before sundown. They were loaded for bear. Bracknell said I'm to be held prisoner to bring pressure to bear on my father.'

'Save the talk for later.' Loman ran his hands over the girl's body and found that she was hogtied. He located the knots and untied them, his gaze busy around the darkened camp.

'They tied me too tightly,' she complained, and

staggered as she gained her feet. 'The ropes have constricted my circulation.'

Loman supported her until she could stand alone.

'I saw Bracknell when the ambusher brought me in here at sundown,' she said. 'He asked me if I had seen any sign of gold around the ranch, and wouldn't believe me when I told him there was none. He rode out with his crew, apart from that guard, and I've no idea where he's gone.'

Loman heard a twig snap close by and whirled swiftly. A dark figure was lunging at him, one arm upraised. Loman pushed Kate to one side and set himself for trouble. He stepped forward swiftly to meet the attack and lend power to his defence. He took the man's punch on his left shoulder and slammed his right fist in a tight arc that snapped against the man's jaw and sent him backwards in a heavy fall.

It was too dark to see with any distinction. The man came up off the ground like a rubber ball and hurtled into Loman, who gained a hazy impression of a big figure whose flailing fists were hard as rocks. The man was tall and wearing a high-crowned Stetson. He was obviously well-versed in fighting, while Loman's own considerable ability had been impaired by his fall earlier.

They fought silently, except for the grunts that accompanied the man's every punch. His heavy fists pounded Loman, who was unusually slow in getting started, but Loman dug hard, using his considerable weight, and was dismayed that the man took everything he had to offer, shaking off the effects, and coming back swinging both fists. A right hand caught Loman on the left cheek, just below the temple that had suffered the impact when his horse had been shot, and Loman's knees unhinged and he sprawled on his face.

A heavy boot crashed into his ribs and he rolled, the movement making him dizzy. He scrambled up, fearing the worst just when he needed to get to grips with the situation. The man came in close again, and a solid knee thudded against Loman's upper thigh as he twisted to protect his belly. His right leg lost all feeling beyond the excruciating pain that flooded it, and he was forced to sway his weight to the left.

Loman backed off, trying to keep out of reach of the hammer-like fists that came in fast to work him over. He rolled his head to the right and hard knuckles grazed his cheek once again, sending a wave of pain through his temple. Lights flickered in his brain and a sickening buzz assailed his ears. A dark shadow seemed to slip before his gaze and he feared he was losing his senses. Desperation welled up in him and he lurched forward, fists flailing. This was one fight he could not afford to lose.

He landed a solid left against the man's chin, driving him back, but a knee slammed into his belly in a murderous counter, and Loman reached out to grab the man and hang on. He took several blows to his ribs, which robbed him of his breath, and fell back defensively, hands weaving slightly as he sought to parry the rain of blows that threatened to finish him. He was aware that he was being hammered into the ground and desperation filled him. His head felt as if he had fallen upon it from the roof of a barn and his senses were unstable.

The fall from his horse had weakened him considerably or he would have beaten the man, but Loman knew instinctively that he was fighting a losing battle. Those mauling fists came at him from all angles, striking like sledge-hammers hitting a fence post. No matter what he did, Loman failed to get the upper hand, and he sensed the end was near. His strength was fading fast and he had no answer to the man's vicious attack.

He took a right to his chin which robbed him of his sense of balance, and was not aware that he had fallen until his face made heavy contact with the hard ground. He rolled over on to his back, in time for the man to come down heavily upon him. He reached up desperately and grabbed the man's shoulders, wincing in anticipation of those slogging fists striking him again, but the man's body was limp, a dead weight upon him, and he became aware of Kate standing over them, a rifle held menacingly in her slim hands, its butt ready for a second blow.

Loman drew a ragged breath into his palpitating lungs. He barely had the strength to push the unconscious man away, and Kate reached down and helped him to his feet.

'You were too bad to be true,' she observed. 'He was killing you!'

'Tell me something I don't know!' he retorted. 'I was half-dead before I started. My head hit a rock when my horse was shot from under me and knocked most of the sense out of me. What happened to you?

Why didn't you step in sooner when you saw me having difficulty?'

'With my bare hands?' she countered. 'Come on, let's get out of here. If Bracknell and his men come back now you won't be able to resist them.'

Loman staggered as he turned to survey the camp.

'We'll need horses,' he said.

'Mine is over that way,' Kate responded, tugging on his arm, 'and so is the guard's horse. Come on. I can hear riders coming.'

Loman paused just long enough to pick up the sound of approaching hoofs, then shook his head to clear it and went for his saddle-bags and Winchester. He followed Kate into the shadows and they came upon two horses nearby, tethered to bushes. The sound of approaching riders came loud and clear through the night, and Loman tensed for more action as they hurriedly prepared to leave, certain that they had run out of time.

EIGHT

Loman dropped behind Kate as they rode out, and the girl headed south at a fast pace. Several riders were moving into the camp from the north, and Loman hoped the noise the newcomers were making would cover the sound of their departing hoofs. They could soon lose themselves in the night, providing they were able to put sufficient distance between themselves and the camp. A gunshot rang out, echoing to the distant horizon, and Loman fancied he heard a slug whining overhead.

He spurred to Kate's side and they pushed on. Kate was heading for Double H, and Loman was content with that. He wanted to get the girl off his hands, and thought she would be safe within the defensive circle of her outfit. The situation had changed considerably in the past hours, and he needed to do some checking up. Major Bracknell was playing a dangerous game that was obviously against the law.

The darkened range was eerie to cross, with just enough light from the moon to illuminate their route. Kate rode without hesitation, and Loman thought she had learned her lesson at last about riding alone. It was near midnight when lights showed in the distance, and Kate slowed her horse imperceptibly.

'Don't tell Dad about any of this,' she pleaded.

'You say that as if you fear I will,' he responded. 'Don't you think this has gone far enough? It's fairly obvious now that someone connected with Bracknell fired that shot at your father. So why the mystery? Only a guilty man would want to conceal the facts. What is your father guilty of?' Loman paused, and then a thought struck him. 'Or is he shielding someone?'

'I don't understand,' Kate protested.

'And there's a lot I don't understand,' Loman said bleakly. 'But I'm sure gonna get to the bottom of it before I'm through. I've been dragged into this and I won't let up now I've got my teeth into it. I think you know a lot more than you're telling me, and if you really care about your father then you'd level with me and help all you can. If you hang on too long the shooting will start, and then it will be too late to do anything except fight.'

'I wish you wouldn't talk like that. You're frightening me.'

'The way you've been acting, I don't think you're afraid of anything, or you're just plain reckless, but lives are at stake and mark my words, it will end in shooting. With a man like Major Bracknell on the other side, you can't expect any mercy.'

They rode on, and a soft challenge came out of

the shadows when they reached the yard. Bill McKay emerged into the open when Kate replied, and came to the head of the girl's horse and grasped the reins.

'Where in hell have you been, Kate?' he demanded angrily. 'I've had half the outfit riding the range looking for you. Why didn't you tell me where you were going? I got enough to do around here without the extra worry of you.'

'I'm sorry, Bill, but I just had to get away for a spell. I promise I won't go off again like that.'

'Too right, you won't.' McKay looked up at Loman, his taut features pale in the moonlight. 'The sheriff was out here just before sundown. He wasn't too pleased when I told him I didn't know where you were.'

'I told you I was going to trail Donovan's horse to find out what happened to him,' Loman retorted. 'Did you tell James that?'

'Yeah, I did. But he was none too pleased. He was looking for you, too, Kate, and the way you treat him – the man you're going to marry – ain't the way to get him to lead you to the altar.'

'We were shot at as we rode out of Bracknell's camp by Poison Creek,' Loman said. 'Kate was being held prisoner there as a lever to be used against her father. We may be followed in here, so you'd better get your crew together and be ready for trouble.'

'The hell you say!' McKay turned quickly and went running across the yard to the bunkhouse.

'I hope you're going to stay put on the spread now,' Loman told Kate.

'Where are you going?' she demanded.

'Into town. I need to make some enquiries.'

'Perhaps I'd better ride with you. I ought to see James and set him straight on a few things.'

'I don't want you along. I'll have my work cut out handling my own business without having you to worry about. James will come out to see you if he needs to.'

'Well, thanks for what you did for me earlier. I don't know what Bracknell would have done if you hadn't showed up when you did.'

'You know he means business, whatever he's got on his mind. You'd better get into the house now and stay put until tomorrow.'

She rode meekly through the gateway and Loman watched her until she vanished into the shadows. A sigh escaped him as he turned his mount, touched spurs to its flanks and headed south, making for Coldwater. As he rode he considered what he knew of the local situation. His own mission was simple – find Leo Slattery and arrest him. But he was caught up in this local business and needed the help of his organization to tie a knot in Major Bracknell's rope.

Dawn was breaking when he sighted Coldwater and rode wearily into the little town. A light was burning in the law office. He reined up at the hitch rack in front of it and stepped down from his saddle. Stretching to ease his muscles, he looked around the silent street, flexing his fingers as he did so. He was unsteady on his feet, and was looking forward to a spell in his blankets but did not think that that eventuality was possible. As he turned to the office the street door was opened from the inside and James Sorgan emerged.

'Ward. I heard hoof beats and hoped it was you. Is Kate with you, by any chance? I was out at Double H last night and she had gone missing again. You rode out following Donovan's tracks, so McKay said. Did you have any luck? Donovan was sent here from Double H in a buckboard. He died around midnight.'

Loman paused in mid-stride, shocked by the news. He sighed heavily, and Sorgan put out a steadying hand as he staggered.

'Hey, there's blood on your face, Ward. Did you find trouble out there? Come into the office and let me check you out. You look like you need a cup of coffee.'

'I've got a lot to tell you.' Loman followed Sorgan into the office. He sat down in the chair beside the desk and tried to relax while the sheriff fetched him some coffee.

Sorgan came back to him and Loman drank deeply of the strong black liquid.

'A wire came for you yesterday afternoon,' Sorgan said. 'Seth, the telegraph operator, asked me if I knew whether there was a Ward Loman in town. I didn't know you're working for the Pinkerton Agency.'

He produced a yellow envelope and handed it over. Loman did not open it. He drank the rest of the coffee and felt better for it.

'The eating-house should be open about now,' he said. 'I need to take in some food before I drop dead from starvation. Come with me and while I eat I'll tell you what's been happening on the range.'

Sorgan nodded and they left the office. The sheriff locked the door and they walked along the street.

'Did Hub Slattery show up in town yesterday?' Loman asked, feeling that the events of the previous day had taken place a long time ago.

Sorgan laughed harshly. 'He sure did, and when he began to threaten me because I wouldn't let his son Wes out of jail I stuck him behind bars. I'll turn him loose later today, when he's cooled down. Is Kate OK? I wish I knew what is going on with her.'

'You and me both,' Loman said. 'Donovan told me he followed Bracknell's wagons to Poison Creek, where he was ambushed by one of Bracknell's riders and shot in the back. Bill McKay told me a little about the trouble at Double H.' Loman explained about the gold shipment that had vanished towards the end of the war. 'The mystery is who stole it, and what happened to it after the war. None of it has turned up anywhere.'

'Bracknell seems to be doing his own thing,' Sorgan mused, 'killing men without reason – and despite what folks thought of Al Donovan, he was working for the law when he was shot. With your evidence against Bracknell, Ward, I reckon we can pick him up now.'

'There's more to it.' Loman went on to narrate the events that led to him being ambushed and the subsequent fight by Bracknell's wagons. 'Bracknell was holding Kate prisoner. He told her he would use her as a lever to put pressure on her father, but I got her out of there and left her safe at Double H.'

They entered the restaurant and Loman ordered breakfast. He sighed with satisfaction when he had eaten his fill, then slaked his thirst with two cups of coffee. He had to fight off tiredness as he fingered his left temple, which was painful.

'You look like hell,' Sorgan said. 'You'd better check with Doc Pearson to see if your cheek-bone is broken. It's swollen, and there's a big cut across your temple.'

Loman grimaced and opened his wire, which was from Allan Pinkerton's Chicago office.

'Well, whaddya know!' he exclaimed. 'This says Leo Slattery was killed in Amarillo four days ago. I'm to report my whereabouts and stand by for fresh orders.'

'So Leo is dead, huh?' Sorgan nodded. 'He was one real bad man who sure needed killing.'

'I've got to talk to Hub Slattery.' Loman pushed himself to his feet. 'I wanta know what happened on that Confederate raid just before the end of the war. Someone got away with the gold, and the trouble hereabouts stems from that.'

Sorgan nodded. 'Let's get to it,' he agreed. 'I'll be mighty satisfied if you can find a reason why Hub should stay on in jail.'

They went out to the street and headed for the law office. Sorgan looked along the street and then broke into a run.

'Looks like trouble at the jail,' he called over his shoulder.

Loman saw several horses standing outside the law

office and ran to keep abreast of Sorgan. A man was standing on the sidewalk beside the horses with a pistol in his hand. The next instant the weapon blasted, and Loman heard a bullet crackle over his head. He drew his pistol, as did Sorgan, and they both fired a single shot. The man fell to the sidewalk and rolled lifeless into the street as heavy echoes raced away across the silent town.

Six horses were standing on the street with trailing reins. Two of them reared up and then ran off out of town. The door of the office was open. A man stuck his head out, looked around, and then pulled back into cover. He reappeared a moment later with a levelled gun, snapped off two quick shots which missed their target, and Sorgan shot him before he could fire again.

Loman held his gun steady as he ran, his tiredness forgotten. His head was aching dully but he ignored the discomfort. They were still twenty yards from the office when six men emerged from it in a tight bunch and ran across the sidewalk to the horses, firing guns at the approaching lawmen. Loman started shooting and Sorgan joined in. Two men fell instantly, and two turned and dashed back into the office. The remaining pair turned to fight and gun smoke flared around them. Moments later they were hit by questing lead from the deadly lawmen and fell. The shooting ceased and echoes grumbled away.

'I'll go into the office,' Sorgan said. 'Go down the alley and watch the back door, Ward. I'll check the office from front to rear.'

Loman nodded and turned into the alley beside

the jail. He slowed to a walk, his shoulders heaving. Sweat was trickling down his face. He was ten yards from the end of the alley when two men rounded the rear corner of the jail. Each was holding a pistol. Loman recognized Hub Slattery and his son Wes, and levelled his gun.

'Hold it,' he called. 'Throw down the guns and put up your hands.'

Hub halted instantly, dropped his gun and raised his hands. Wes lifted his pistol to resist and Loman fired, aiming for the right shoulder. His gun blasted and the bullet smacked into Wes, knocking him sideways against his father. Hub grabbed his son and lowered him to the ground. Loman went forward, gun uplifted.

'You've killed him,' Hub grated. 'You've killed my boy.'

'He ain't dead,' Loman replied. 'I aimed for his shoulder. I want him alive, not dead. Get to your feet. We'll take him back to his cell and I'll have the doctor over to check him out.'

Sorgan appeared around the corner, having emerged from the rear door of the jail. His gun was ready, and he grinned when he saw the situation.

'Hub, pick up Wes and take him back into the jail,' he said. 'Is he still alive? You should have killed the punk, Ward.'

Hub struggled to carry his son back into the cell block, and Wes was placed on a bunk. Loman examined the youngster under Hub Slattery's intent gaze while Sorgan went out for the doctor.

'I told you he'd live,' Loman said eventually. 'He'll

be all right. Who were the men who busted you out of here?'

'Some of my outfit.' Hub's face was pale, his dark eyes filled with shock. 'And they didn't do it on my orders. I don't need the trouble of a jailbreak on my record. I don't have the stomach for fighting against the law.'

'It's a pity you didn't bring your sons up to be the same.' Loman sighed heavily. 'I've got some bad news for you. Your son Leo was killed in Amarillo a few days ago.'

'Leo? Killed?' Slattery sat down on the end of a bunk, shattered by the news. His mouth gaped for a moment and a ghastly expression flitted across his face. 'I don't believe it,' he muttered, shaking his head. 'Not Leo.' He pushed back his shoulders. 'Who said he was killed? I was expecting him at the ranch any day. He's been away for years.'

Loman produced his wire and gave it to the HS rancher to read. Hub gazed at it for a long time, and Loman did not interrupt his thoughts. Then Hub returned the wire to Loman, shaking his head.

'It was Bracknell's doing,' he muttered. 'He said he'd have Leo killed if I didn't toe the line. I thought he was bluffing but he's done it. To hell with that gold! It's caused nothing but trouble.' He looked up at Loman, his face pinched, ashen, his eyes blazing with an unholy light. 'You got to let me outa here,' he rapped. 'I wanta kill Bracknell.'

'I'm sorry,' Loman said softly. 'I was sent here to arrest Leo if he showed up. He was wanted for killing a town marshal in San Antonio last year.'

'Leo didn't kill that marshal. He wrote me about it. He was framed by Bracknell, who wanted a hold over me.' He paused, frowning, and then asked: 'Who are you? How'd you get that wire?'

'I'm a Pinkerton detective.' Loman looked up as Sorgan walked into the cell block, followed by Doc Pearson. 'Come into the office, Hub, and sit down. I need to ask you some questions about Major Bracknell. One of his men shot Al Donovan in the back, and I want Bracknell for that. Leave the doc to do his stuff with Wes. I've told you he'll live.'

Hub walked through to the front office and sat down on the chair beside the desk. Loman could smell gun smoke in the big room as he faced the rancher.

'What did you mean about Bracknell having a lot to answer for?' he asked.

Slattery's harshly set face was grey with shock. He shook his head.

'I should have had the guts to kill Bracknell years ago. He's been at the back of my trouble from the day I met him. I always reckoned I'd have to kill him one day, and if I had done it years ago, Leo would be alive now.'

'Tell me about it,' Loman urged.

'I told you Leo was framed with killing the marshal by Bracknell's men. Some of them were in my outfit, acting on Bracknell's orders – men he commanded in the army during the war. I was at West Point with Bracknell years before the war.' Slattery shook his head. 'It's hard to believe the way he manipulated everyone there. I passed out as an officer and, being a Southerner, I came to Texas on duty. When the South rebelled against the North I joined the Confederates and fought in the war against the Union. Bracknell was a Yankee Blue-Belly, and became a spy. I saw him behind our lines, and should have had him shot then, but he had a couple of bad things against me and blackmailed me into letting him go.'

Slattery lapsed into silence, and Loman waited patiently.

'So you let him go,' he hinted.

'Yeah, and it was the worst day's work I ever did. He showed up again later, with papers which falsely proved I'd been working for the Yankees as a spy. He was gonna frame me if I didn't go along with his plans, and I would have been shot as a traitor. The war was grinding to an end then, and Bracknell told me about the gold shipment. I passed the word to my superiors and they organized the raid. I expected to command the raiding party, but Henry Hesp got it. Henry and I were good friends in those days. I offered to take his place on the raid, but then I was detailed to lead a supporting patrol, and I managed to get to the gold before Hesp did.'

'So what happened,' Loman persisted when Slattery fell silent.

'I'd rather not talk about that.' Slattery leaned forward, put his elbows on the desk and pushed his face into his cupped hands.

Loman gave him a few moments, and then grasped his shoulder.

'You're gonna have to tell me the truth sooner or

later, Hub, so do it now, and then I can arrest Bracknell. You wouldn't want him to get away, would you?'

Slattery looked up. 'Bracknell captured my patrol. We arranged it. My men were taken as prisoners of war and Bracknell replaced them with his own men. I carried out the raid leading a bunch of Yankees dressed as rebels! After I took the gold I hid it, and Bracknell killed the men of the patrol to close their mouths. He would have killed me along with them but I wouldn't tell him where the gold was hidden. He let me go, figuring to blackmail me into handing it over after the war ended. But he didn't know about Hesp's patrol. When Hesp showed up I told him the gold boxes contained nothing but sand and rocks. He took one look and rode out fast, fearing a trap, and I rode with him back to our lines. The war ended shortly after that.'

'So what caused the bad blood between you and Hesp?' Loman noticed that Sorgan had come out of the cell block and was listening to Slattery's confession.

'I came back to this range and bought my spread with some of the gold. Hesp took over Double H when his father died, and I guess he never really believed my story about there being no gold shipment because he cut me dead. Then Bracknell turned up, wanting the gold, and I was in a cleft stick. While Bracknell couldn't get his hands on the gold he wouldn't kill me. I've managed to keep him at bay, but now he's had Leo killed, and I'll see him in hell before he gets hold of a single grain of gold.'

'Where is the gold hidden?' Loman asked.

Slattery smiled. 'I reckon I'll take that secret to my grave,' he said.

'It would be in your favour to tell us where it is,' Sorgan said. 'I'd turn you loose the minute we got hold of the gold, no matter what you've done.'

'You got nothing to hold me for,' Slattery retorted. 'Turn me loose now and I'll kill Bracknell.'

'You took that gold in the line of duty,' Sorgan said, 'but by your own admission you stole it and didn't return it to the authorities. You may not look upon that as a crime, but I'm holding you until that gold is back where it belongs. Tell me where it is now and I'll overlook the fact that you used some of it to buy your spread. You can cut your losses now, Hub, and put Bracknell where he belongs.'

'Let me go so I can kill Bracknell, and I'll hand over the gold afterwards,' Slattery said stubbornly.

'You'll be better off in jail until we've got Bracknell,' Loman said.

'No deal.' Slattery glared at them, and Loman could tell he would not change his mind.

'I have to send a wire to my headquarters,' Loman said to Sorgan. 'Then I'll need to wait for a reply. I'll stick around town until I get new orders, James. Maybe you'd better ride out to Double H and check that Kate is OK. Bracknell sure wanted to get his hands on her. He must think her father knows where the gold is.'

'Hesp knows nothing about it,' Slattery said dully. 'I knew years ago that he was too honest for his own good. If he'd known what I did on that raid he would have spilled it to our superiors.'

'That's good enough for me.' Loman nodded. 'I need to set the wires buzzing. You could get Hub's story down on paper while I'm making contact with my office, James.'

'Sure thing,' Sorgan replied.

Loman went to the door, his mind working on the statement Slattery had made. He departed, and the instant he cleared the doorway of the office several guns opened fire at him from across the street. . . .

NINE

Loman hurled himself sideways to the left as a slug tore through the crown of his hat. His pistol, cocked and ready for action, was in his hand before his left shoulder hit the dusty boards of the sidewalk. He triggered the weapon at three grim figures, wreathed in gunsmoke, standing across the street and fanning their pistols to hurl a torrent of hot lead at him. Bullets slammed into the front wall of the office as the raucous sounds of the shooting hammered out the silence.

A slug bored through the holster on Loman's right hip and another gouged his left forearm just below the elbow, leaving a stab of agony on his flesh in passing. He fired at the centre man of the trio, his eyes narrowed against flaring gunsmoke. The man went down as if his legs had been kicked from under him.

Loman shifted his aim and put a slug through the chest of the man on the right, who spun around and fell heavily on his face in the dust of the street. The third man turned and ran into the alley mouth opposite, paused to fire a last shot in Loman's direction, then disappeared. The shooting ceased and gunsmoke drifted.

The office door was opened and Sorgan appeared framed in the aperture, gun in hand. Loman got to his feet.

'Are you OK, Ward?' Sorgan demanded.

'I think so.' Loman glanced around the street before glancing at his left arm. He saw blood seeping into the fabric of his shirt and shook his head. 'I got nicked,' he added. 'It looks like the war has started, huh?'

'I reckon to get a posse, head out to Poison Creek and pick up Bracknell and his bunch.' Sorgan holstered his pistol. 'Can I count on you to ride with me?'

'I must send a wire to my head office in Chicago without delay, and then wait for a reply which will contain fresh orders. That's the way we work, James.'

'Better get that under way right now. I'd like to have you with me. It could get tricky trying to take Bracknell with a deputy US marshal in his crew.'

'I'm doubtful of that guy being genuine.' Loman shook his head. 'Let's take a look at those two men I downed. The third one got clear, and I'm tempted to go for him, but he'll wait, huh?'

They crossed the street and stood over the two figures sprawled in the dust.

'I've seen this one before.' Sorgan toed one of the bodies. 'I'm sure he was with Bracknell when those wagons first pulled in.'

Loman turned away. 'I'll be back shortly,' he said in parting.

He went along the street to the telegraph office, composed a report, and handed it to the operator.

'I'll expect a reply this afternoon,' he said. 'If it comes before I get back to collect it you can deliver it to the law office.'

'Sure thing.' The operator sat down at his sending-key and began to tap out the message. Loman watched for a moment before departing. He looked around the street before stepping out from the cover of the doorway. His nerves were taut as he returned to the law office.

Sorgan was in the cell block, talking to his prisoners when Loman reached him. The sheriff was not pleased, judging by the expression on his face. He ushered Loman into the office and locked the door connecting the office to the cells.

'I can't get anything from either Aird or Bellamy about that business in the alley with Kate,' Sorgan said angrily. 'What makes it worse is that Kate ain't told the truth about it either. I'll keep those two locked away until hell freezes over if they don't change their minds and start spouting the truth. Apart from that, Hub Slattery is driving me over the edge with his whining about getting turned loose, but I'll hold him until after I've got Bracknell and his outfit in here, just in case something comes up that implicates Slattery. How'd you get on? Send off your wire OK?'

Loman nodded. 'Yeah, and I've got to wait for a reply before I make a move,' he said.

'Will you stand by here for me so I can ride out with a posse? I need to hit the trail fast and take those buzzards with the wagons before they know what's doing.'

'Sure. I'm hogtied until I get a reply from my office, and it might not arrive today. I can hold the fort until you get back.'

'Thanks, Ward. You're a pal. I'll split the breeze pronto. The posse will be gathering down at the livery stable right now. See you when I get that job done.'

Loman nodded and walked to the street door to watch Sorgan's departure. The sheriff hurried along the sidewalk to the stable, disappeared inside, and then reappeared moments later astride a white horse. He was followed by ten possemen. The party came along the street and rode swiftly out of town, heading north. Loman watched them out of sight, and when he tasted the dust drifting across the street from the hoofs of the riders he closed the street door.

Tiredness was tugging at Loman's senses. His left forearm was smarting. He examined the superficial wound and poured water on it from a bucket standing on a side table, using a dipper hanging down the side. The pain did not decrease and he decided to check with the doctor later. He sat down behind the desk and tried to interest himself in some of the paperwork lying there, but soon put his elbows on the desk and lowered his head into his hands.

He fell asleep without meaning to, and awoke later to find someone shaking his shoulder. He opened his eyes and stifled a yawn. The telegraph operator was standing over him, waving a yellow envelope in his hand.

'Your reply,' the man said, turning away when Loman took the envelope. He departed quickly, and Loman scanned the mesage, which read:

LOMAN. COLDWATER, TEXAS. NEW ASSIGNMENT: LOCATE AND ARREST MAN BELIEVED TO BE IN YOUR AREA KNOWN AS MAJOR BRACKNELL, WANTED FOR MURDER AND GRAND LARCENY. ALSO BEN LACEY, GUNMAN POSING AS DEPUTY US MARSHAL. INVESTIGATE CONSIGNMENT OF GOLD STOLEN FIVE YEARS AGO FROM US BANK IN BRETTVILLE AND NEVER RECOVERED. GOOD LUCK. SOURCE AND ORIGIN: T.J. MARSTON, HEAD OFFICE, PINKERTON DETECTIVE AGENCY, CHICAGO.

Loman read the message twice and then got to his feet to pace the office. He was intrigued by the information that Ben Lacey was merely posing as a federal lawman, for he'd had reservations about the man. He tucked the message into a breast pocket, went into the cell block and confronted Hub Slattery. The HS rancher got up off his bunk and came to the barred door.

'Are you gonna turn me loose now?' Slattery shook the bars impatiently. 'Bracknell could be getting away right now, and I wanta see him through gunsmoke.'

'You know he won't leave until he's got his hands on that gold,' Loman said. 'When was the last time you saw Bracknell?'

'I've seen him too damn often recently. Let me outa here so I can kill him. I ain't committed an offence. You can't hold me for nothing.'

'I'm not the sheriff, and he's left town right now. You'll have to take it up with him when he returns.'

Slattery turned away, muttering angrily, and sat down on a corner of his bunk. Loman studied the man for a few moments, wanting more information but aware that he would learn nothing while Slattery was in his present mood. He turned to look at the other prisoners, and went to the door of the cell containing Cal Frazee. The big man glared at him but said nothing. His dark eyes were filled with the watchfulness of a cornered wild animal.

'Why did you shoot Joel Bender?' Loman asked.

'He was up to no good, nosing around the major's wagons.'

'You know that's not a lawful reason for killing a man. It was cold-blooded murder. Why did you do it?'

'I had orders from the major to shoot anyone who tried to interfere. If you don't like what happened then talk to Bracknell about it.'

'You're an ex-soldier who always obeys the last order, huh?'

'That's right. It don't matter to me if the order is right or wrong. I get an order – I carry it out.'

'What do you know about the missing gold shipment stolen from Brettville in the last weeks of the war?'

'No more than anyone else. I heard about it, and that's all.'

'You don't know that Bracknell is in this area trying to locate that gold, huh?'

Frazee's weathered face broke into a grin.

'I don't ask the major his business. Why don't you brace him about it?'

'I will when I get my hands on him,' Loman responded. 'Tell me about Ben Lacey.'

'He's a federal lawman. I never had anything to do with him.' Frazee shrugged.

Loman gave up and went back into the front office. He was impatient to get to work on his new assignment, and wished Sorgan had not left him with the responsibility of the jail and its occupants. He heard hoof beats on the street and went to the street door, for there was a sound of urgency about the approaching rider that alerted him. He opened the door and peered outside. A groan escaped him when he saw Kate Hesp riding along the street hell for leather. He had hoped he'd seen the last of her until this business was settled. Then he spotted a rider behind Kate, chasing fast with an uplifted six-gun in his right hand.

Loman drew his pistol and fired a shot as the man levelled his weapon to fire at Kate. The thunderclap of the gunshot startled the town and chased out the silence. The pursuer pitched sideways out of his saddle. Loman wrinkled his nose against the drifting gunsmoke enveloping him and faced Kate as she reined into the sidewalk where he was standing. She seemed badly shocked. Her slim shoulders were heaving. Her face was pale, her eyes filled with fear. She tried to dismount but came sprawling out of the saddle. Loman stepped in close to catch her.

'What's going on, Kate?' he demanded, setting her on her feet and steadying her.

'Bracknell rode into Double H early this morning with about ten men. There was a lot of shooting. I was returning from a morning ride and saw the whole thing happening from a distance. Then I was spotted and had to ride out fast.' She glanced over her shoulder at the motionless figure sprawled in the street. 'He chased me all the way to town. I didn't think I would make it. Thank heaven you were here.'

'James isn't here. He rode out to Poison Creek with a posse to pick up Bracknell and his men.' Loman shook his head. 'With any luck he'll drop in at Double H on the way.'

'I didn't see him on the trail.' Kate spoke wearily. She was trembling in shock, her voice wavering. 'He must have headed directly to Poison Creek, which would have taken him five miles to the west of the ranch.' She staggered as she turned, and Loman supported her with his left arm.

'Have you any friends in town you can stay with until this is over?' he asked, his thoughts ranging over the situation.

'I'm staying just long enough to get a fresh horse from the livery stable and then I'll be riding back to the ranch,' she replied firmly.

'That wouldn't be a good idea. I'm stuck here until James returns, and then I'll be taking the trail.' Loman looked around the street. A few men who had ventured out to check on the shots were gathering around the dead man. One of them was Frank Mason, the town mayor. Mason was looking in Loman's direction and Loman beckoned the man to join him. 'Can you round up a couple of dependable men who would handle the law office until the sheriff gets back?' he asked. 'I have to ride out and there are prisoners in the cells.'

'Cole Amson works as the town jailer when required,' Mason said. 'I'll tell him you need him.'

'Thanks, and make it quick, will you? There's trouble out at Double H, and I need to get on the trail.'

Mason hurried off along the street. Loman took Kate into the office and the girl slumped into a seat. Loman sat down behind the desk.

'I wouldn't want you to leave town before I ride out to Double H,' he told her. 'Try not to worry. I doubt if Bracknell will want to harm your father. The man he's really interested in is Hub Slattery, who's safely in jail.'

A side window overlooking the alley beside the office suddenly shattered. Glass flew as Loman hurled himself sideways off the chair in a reflex action. He landed behind the desk and rolled, drawing his pistol and cocking the weapon as he surged upright. An indistinct figure was at the window, thrusting the muzzle of a revolver into the office, and Loman's pistol blasted as the man triggered his gun.

The office shook to the thunder of exploding weapons. Loman had no time to look out for Kate. He sent two shots at the window, aware of splinters leaping up out of the top of the desk as two slugs came in search of his flesh. The man outside faded away, struck by a single shot, and Loman was temporarily deafened by the shooting. His ears rang in protest at the raucous disturbance and gunsmoke stung his nostrils.

Kate was frozen in her seat, her ashen face betraying horror. Loman moved to the side window and peered out. He saw a man lying dead in the alley. At that moment the street door was thrust open violently and two men came bursting into the office, guns in their hands.

Loman triggered his Colt, lunging forward as he did so to tip Kate off her chair. He dropped to one knee as she went sprawling, his narrowed eyes noting that the foremost of the two gunmen was spilling his gun from his hand as he went down heavily on the threshold. The second man's view of the office was obstructed by his dying sidekick. Loman drew a bead on the man's chest and rocked the office with another hammering shot.

The man fired once, his gun blasting a shot into the floorboards as he fell forward on his face. Loman restrained his breathing against the smoke drifting around the office and ran to the door, his gun uplifted and ready. He risked a glance outside, saw that there were no more assailants, and took a quick breath of clean air. He turned to inspect the men although he was aware that he had killed both of them. Kate was getting up off the floor, rubbing her right elbow as she gazed at him.

'I never saw anything like that before,' she said in a shocked whisper. 'You're faster even than James and I didn't think anyone could shade him.'

She picked up the chair she had been sitting on and dropped on to it with a sigh of relief, then leaned forward, put her arms on the desk and lowered her head. The next instant she was sobbing in shock.

Loman watched her for a moment. His face was set in grim lines. There was nagging impatience in him because he needed to be on the move. A voice hailed the office from outside and he turned swiftly, expecting more shooting.

'Hello, the office. I'm Amson the jailer. What's going on?'

Loman risked a glance from the doorway and saw a big, square-shouldered man standing alone in the street. He was carrying a Winchester rifle cradled in his right arm and wore a gun belt with a holstered pistol on his right hip. His big face bore an expression of alertness and he gazed at Loman without moving.

'I'm Ward Loman, deputy sheriff and Pinkerton detective. I've got prisoners in the cells and I need to ride out pronto. Come on in and we'll get acquainted. Do you see any strangers around the street who might be intent on busting in here?'

'Not now.' Armstrong came forward slowly. 'I saw six men riding by as I came this way. Three turned off into Harper's Alley. Of the other three, one went into the alley beside the jail and the other two came to the front door. It looks like you've taken care of them.'

Loman dragged the two dead men out of the office and left them in the street. He looked around with keen gaze, and spotted a man holding a six-gun peering out of an alley some twenty yards to the right. He stepped back into the office, having recognized the man as Ben Lacey, the alleged deputy US marshal who was travelling with Bracknell.

'The trouble here isn't over yet,' he said. 'Those other three men are coming now, it looks like, and one of them is Ben Lacey.'

'He wasn't with Bracknell at the ranch this morning,' Kate said. 'What can we do, Ward?'

'Wait for him to get here,' Loman said quietly. 'Amson, go into the cells and stand guard there. Take Kate with you, and make sure she stays put with her head down. I'll handle the street out front.'

Amson nodded and picked up the bunch of cell keys. He ushered Kate into the cell block. Loman followed to get a look at the interior of the cells. There was a stout wooden door at the rear and a long, narrow window in a side wall, very high up and offering no view of the interior. He moved back into the office and faced the street door, standing against the wall on the left where he also had a good view of the shattered side window overlooking the alley.

Loman checked his gun, ejecting spent cartridges from the cylinder and reloading with fresh shells from the loops on his belt. It was not his move, and he waited silently, his impatience gone, swept away by the advent of action.

TEN

Loman did not move as tense moments passed. Silence hung heavily over the office, accompanied by an unnerving stillness. His gun was in his right hand and every nerve seemed to be on edge as he waited. He heard a slight metallic sound outside the alley window, as if someone had accidentally knocked a drawn weapon against the wall. He hunched a little – unconsciously adopting the gunman's crouch, and waited stoically. The time for hard action had arrived.

A head showed at the side window and Loman covered it, half his attention remaining on the front door. When a hand holding a gun came through the broken window he fired a shot at the head, which was hastily withdrawn. He heard the sound of movement at the street door, although nothing showed there.

'Hold your fire in the office,' a harsh voice commanded. 'This is Ben Lacey, deputy US marshal. What's going on here?'

Loman grinned. Here was a chance he rarely encountered in his line of work – one of the principal members of the opposition walking straight into a showdown unaware that his cover was blown.

'I'm Ward Loman, deputy sheriff,' he replied. 'Come in, Marshal. The shooting is about over for now.'

A shadow appeared on the boardwalk outside the doorway and paused there, foreshortened by the height of the sun overhead.

'I want you to come out,' Lacey replied harshly. 'My brand of the law is the highest in the country, so do as I say. I'm taking over here and I want to use your office as my headquarters. There is trouble on the range that you have no idea of so come on out. I need to get to work. There is a lot at stake, and we don't want a tragedy here of lawman fighting lawman.'

'I have responsibilities I can't ignore,' Loman replied. 'I've given you the invitation to come in. Take it or get to hell out and come back when the sheriff is here.'

'Sorgan is not coming back,' Lacey replied in a chill tone. 'When I confronted him earlier, he elected to fight and I had to kill him. He's gone, and I aim to take over in his place.'

Loman felt a stab of disbelief inside as he took in Lacey's words. Sorgan was dead? He doubted that. He didn't think there was a man alive who could beat the sheriff in a straight confrontation. But Lacey would not have given Sorgan an even break, and James would not have known that Lacey was a fraud.

'Lacey, I know you're not a US marshal. I got a wire from the Pinkerton Agency in Chicago about

Bracknell and you. I'm a Pinkerton man, and my orders are to arrest you and the major. I don't know exactly what your crooked business is, but I can tell you that it is over as of now. Disarm yourself and walk into the office or I'll come out and take you.'

A silence followed Loman's words and he waited, watching door and side window. The shadow remained on the boardwalk for some moments, and then it moved backwards quickly and was gone. Loman lunged forward and dived out through the doorway, going low and rolling across the sidewalk to land in the dust of the street. He came up to one knee, gun lifting, his narrowed gaze sweeping around for sign of the opposition.

The tall figure of Ben Lacey was fading into the mouth of the alley beside the jail. Loman fired instantly. Splinters flew from the corner of the building. A gun blasted at him from somewhere across the street and he flattened out and sent a slug speeding in reply at a figure made indistinct by flaring gunsmoke. The man staggered, then pitched forward on to his face in the street. Loman was on his feet and running to the alley where Lacey had vanished before the echoes of the shot could fade.

Lacey was half-way along the alley to the back lots. Loman fired and Lacey broke his long stride. He fell against the wall of the cell block, and then came spinning around to level his upraised pistol. Loman fired again. Lacey took the slug in the centre of his chest and blood spurted. He fell sideways against a wall for support, his mouth gaping, his pistol suddenly too heavy to hold. It dragged out of his hand and thudded in the dust. He came forward a pace on legs that were rapidly losing their strength, and then pitched forward like a tree coming down in a storm.

A gun was fired from the rear of the alley and Loman ducked as a slug snarled by his head. He triggered a shot at the faint movement back there, but the opposition faded away, no doubt unnerved by Lacey's abrupt exit from the fight. Loman stepped back out of the alley and returned to the law office, reloading his gun as he did so. He found Amson covering him from the doorway of the cell block. The jailer lowered his gun and came forward.

'You killed Lacey?' he demanded. 'I heard what passed between you. Is it true that Sorgan is dead?'

'I don't know if there's any truth in what Lacey said, and I can't question him about that or anything else.' Loman saw Kate emerging from the cells, hands to her face. She staggered to a chair and dropped heavily into it, crying softly.

'There may not be any truth in what Lacey said.' Loman spoke through his teeth. 'James was with a posse, and you didn't see him anywhere on the trail so I think Lacey was bluffing. I'm gonna ride out now, and I'm going to Double H to pick up Bracknell. I'll take Hub Slattery with me. I think he holds the answers to what is going on around here. Fetch him out of the cells, Amson, and I'll split the breeze pronto.'

'Sure thing.' The jailer went into the cell block, jangling the bunch of keys.

'I'll ride with you,' Kate said in a whisper. 'I can't stay here. I don't know what Bracknell planned to do out at the ranch, but I'm worried about my father. He is so ill.'

'OK.' Loman nodded. 'I guess you'll be safer in my company than staying in town. But if there's trouble anywhere on the trail then duck and keep low until it is over.'

'I promise,' she said miserably.

Amson returned with Hub Slattery, whose face was alive with question.

'Is it true?' he demanded. 'Is Ben Lacey dead?'

'He's lying stretched out in the alley,' Loman responded. 'Bracknell was seen at Double H earlier and I'm riding out there now to get him dead or alive. You seem to hold some of the answers to what Bracknell wants so I'll take you along with me. Don't make the mistake of trying to escape. I'm not in the habit of losing a prisoner once I've got him, and those that try to get away usually wind up dead.'

'I'll go along with you,' Slattery said eagerly. 'I wanta see the end of this business. It's been going on too long. I was a fool ever to get involved, but Bracknell was blackmailing me and I had to go along with him. I know it was wrong, and my weakness has resulted in my boy Leo getting murdered. Now I wanta finish it.'

'I'll arrest Bracknell if I can, or kill him if I can't take him peaceable. You'll stay out of it. What I want from you is information, so we'll talk as we ride. Bracknell wants that gold, and he hasn't got it yet or he'd be long gone from this range. That leaves you and Henry Hesp, and one of you must know where the gold is.'

'I don't know where it is.' Slattery lips were pinched. 'I wouldn't touch it now. My boy's blood is on it.'

'Let's get moving.' Loman spoke impatiently. 'Stick close to me, and if you look like you're trying to slide off I'll put a bullet in you. Kate, stay close behind.'

He left the office and started for the livery stable, gun in hand, gaze sweeping his surroundings, aware that there were one or two of Bracknell's men loose, but their knowledge that he had killed Ben Lacey should have choked their appetite for bracing him. Kate led her horse and they reached the barn without incident. Moments later they were mounted and riding out of town. Loman set a fast pace, and now his mind was leaping ahead to what might be awaiting him at Double H.

Kate rode several yards behind Loman, who kept Hub Slattery on his left. Loman checked the tracks left by the posse that had ridden out with Sorgan, and paused when he saw where they had branched off the trail to the left and headed into the desolation of the range.

'Look at those tracks,' he said to Kate. 'That's where James turned off with the posse. If Lacey followed you from Double H then there was no way he could have set eyes on James today.'

Kate nodded, although her expression indicated that she was not impressed by the facts.

'So what happened on that raid to steal the gold?' Loman asked as they continued. 'From what I've learned I assume that Henry Hesp led one patrol and you commanded another. You met Bracknell on the way and your patrol was captured as arranged by Bracknell, your men being replaced by Union soldiers dressed in Confederate uniforms. You got to Brettville first, removed the gold, and when Hesp turned up with his patrol you showed him the gold boxes filled with stones and sand.'

'That was the plan Bracknell had worked out, but he tricked everyone right along the line. I emptied those boxes, took my share of the gold and hid it. The rest was shipped south in a couple of wagons driven by Bracknell's men – Union soldiers in Union territory. That was the last I saw of it. But the bulk of the gold never reached the rendezvous Bracknell had arranged, although I didn't know that at the time. I rode back to our lines with Hesp and his patrol and made a report on the raid. When the war ended, I recovered the gold I had hidden and paid off the mortgage on my ranch. I reckoned Bracknell had got the rest and kept it for himself, but he caught up with me about a year ago and came asking for it.'

'And you had no idea where it went after you saw it leaving with Bracknell's men after the raid?' Loman persisted.

'That's right. I was shocked when Bracknell told me. I couldn't help him at all. I pointed out that his men had left with the gold so he should start asking questions of them. He said they were all killed while taking the gold to the rendezvous and no trace of the shipment was seen again. I was the only one who got away with any of it. Bracknell reckoned I had double-crossed him. He wouldn't believe my version of what happened.'

They rode on, and Loman considered Slattery's statement.

'Hesp also believed you'd taken the gold,' he mused. 'That's the reason why you two fell out, huh?'

'It was, as far as I know. He accused me of beating him to the gold and stealing it before he arrived. I told him I thought he'd beaten me to it, removed it, rode off, and then returned later to fool me into thinking I had beaten him there. That little ruse cleared him of any suspicion of being involved in the disappearance of the gold, and left me as the main suspect.'

'Let it rest there,' Loman decided. 'When I pick up Bracknell, we'll get together with Hesp and thrash this out.'

But Loman could not let that matter rest. He questioned Slattery intermittently as they rode to Double H, but learned nothing more beyond the fact that Bracknell had taken to terrorizing both Slattery and Hesp in an endeavour to break them and retrieve the gold.

'So Bracknell is responsible for the rustling and trouble that's been going on around here,' Loman said at last. 'He had Hesp ambushed, huh? But he didn't want him killed, just frightened. It didn't work though. Hesp doesn't know what happened to the gold. He never even saw it. You did, Slattery, and you want me to believe that it slipped through your fingers, apart from your share.'

'You can believe what you like,' Slattery said

angrily. 'I've told you the truth. What you think about it is your business.'

They continued until Double H showed ahead. Loman noticed a trace of smoke in the sky. He rode up an incline to a ridge and peered out over the range to where the cattle ranch was spread out before him. He saw that a barn had burned down, and there were men in the yard, milling around as if they had no idea what to do. There were no sounds of shooting, however, and Loman pushed his mount into a lope towards the spread.

'Slattery,' he called. 'Ride with Kate and stay several yards behind.'

Loman loosened his pistol in its holster as he entered the yard. He saw Bill McKay standing by a corral. The foreman's right shoulder was heavily bandaged. Loman went forward and reined up in front of the ranch foreman.

'What happened here?' he demanded. 'Where are Bracknell and his bunch? I heard they were here early this morning.'

'Yeah, he hit us with a dozen men.' McKay spotted Kate and surprise filled his tone. 'You went riding again, when you were told not to leave the spread.'

'It's a good thing I did,' Kate replied. 'I saw Bracknell riding in with his men as I was returning, and managed to get away to town without being caught.'

'So what happened?' Loman persisted. 'Did Bracknell get in here?'

'No. We beat him off, but the boss told me to let Bracknell into the house for a talk. Bracknell stayed about an hour and then left, taking his men with him. He headed out towards Poison Creek, and I let him go. There was no point fighting him. I had to take care of this place.'

'Was Ben Lacey with Bracknell?' Loman asked.

McKay shook his head. 'I never saw him. He must have been raising hell some place else when Bracknell rode in here.'

'Has Sorgan showed up today?' Loman continued.

Again McKay shook his head.

'I'll ride over to Poison Creek,' Loman decided. 'You'll come with me, Slattery. Kate, remain here and keep your head down.'

The girl dismounted, left her horse standing with trailing reins, and hurried across the yard towards the house. Loman swung his horse around and rode to the gate, accompanied by Slattery. They left the ranch at a canter. Loman saw tracks of horses heading in the same direction and kept an eye on them as he proceeded.

They rode to Poison Creek, and Loman reined in when he saw Bracknell's two wagons drawn up beside the brackish water. There was no sign of life and he rode in cautiously, gun drawn. He saw Bracknell's tracks leading straight by the camp without stopping, and concentrated on the figures sprawled on the ground around the second wagon. He was tight-lipped, fearing the worst as he closed in, for the first man he came across was James Sorgan, lying on his back with arms outstretched. Shock hit Loman hard as he slid out of his saddle.

But Sorgan, hit in the lower chest, was alive, and

Loman worked on him, cleansing his wound and pouring drops of water into his mouth. Sorgan groaned. His eyes flickered open and he peered at Loman. A faint smile came to his lips as recognition flared in his eyes.

'You'll be OK, James,' Loman told him, glancing around at the other bodies. Slattery was checking them for survivors. 'What happened here?'

'We walked into an ambush. I thought the camp was deserted and we came in openly, but Lacey was here with several men, and they fired at us without warning. It was a helluva way for a deputy US marshal to act, huh?'

'Lacey's dead,' Loman told him. 'He came into town and tried to take over, but I'd got a wire from headquarters telling me Lacey was not connected with the law – is a gunman working with Bracknell, who isn't working for the US government. Bracknell was at Double H around dawn this morning, and rode back this way later. I figure he's gone on to Slattery's place. His tracks are heading there.'

'This business about the missing gold shipment.' Sorgan stifled a groan. 'I knew nothing about it.'

'I'm picking up information about it as I go along,' Loman said. 'I got orders to arrest Bracknell so I'll take out after him now. I'll have to leave you here, James, until I can get back to you.'

'Sure. I'll be OK,' the sheriff muttered, and slipped into unconsciousness.

Loman arose, alerted by a shouted warning from Slattery. A rider was approaching from the direction of Double H. Loman sighed when he recognized

Kate riding in, but this time he was not angered by her appearance.

He confronted Kate as she dismounted, warning her of Sorgan's condition. She hurried to the sheriff's side. Slattery helped Loman to move Sorgan into the shade of a wagon and they made him comfortable.

'I'm riding over to HS,' Loman said. 'You'll have to cope here alone, Kate.'

'Make sure you kill Bracknell when you get him in your sights,' she said.

Loman signalled to Slattery and they mounted and rode on in the direction of HS. The tracks of half a dozen horses showed clearly on the ground. Loman pushed his horse along at a fast clip, intent on getting Bracknell in his sights.

'Why is Bracknell hanging around your place, Slattery?' he demanded. 'He must know something, and he sure believes you know where that gold is. He ain't the kind of man to work on hunches. He's got certain knowledge of what happened to the gold shipment.'

'I never got it,' Slattery retorted. 'It's a big mystery to me.'

They rode on until the HS ranch came into sight. Smoke was rising raggedly from a burning building, curling away into the bright blue sky in black, uneven billows. Loman reined in when he heard the sound of shooting coming from the spread.

'Looks like your outfit is resisting Bracknell,' Loman observed.

'Just a handful of them,' Slattery said. 'Bracknell got some of his men hired in amongst my crew and they were watching me. I flushed them out yesterday, but Bracknell won't give up. I'm gonna have to kill him to stop him. I've been a fool, pussyfooting with him. Leo would still be alive if I'd shot Bracknell first off.'

'I want him alive,' Loman said firmly.

'You're gonna need me to help you take his bunch,' Slattery observed with a crooked grin. 'Let's play it as the cards fall, huh?'

The sounds of shooting dwindled away and an ominous silence settled over the ranch. Loman pulled a pair of field glasses from a saddle-bag and adjusted them to his sight. He studied the ranch and saw men moving around. Bracknell was standing on the porch of the ranch house, looking around, a gun in his hand. Two men emerged from the bunkhouse dragging a third man between them. Loman watched intently. The prisoner was hauled before Bracknell, who questioned him. Moments later Bracknell fired a shot and the prisoner slumped to the ground.

'It looks like Bracknell ain't taking prisoners,' Loman observed. 'He's sure got a one-track mind where that gold is concerned.'

'Why don't we ride in there and finish him off before anyone else is killed?' Slattery demanded.

'That is my intention,' Loman replied, 'but you're not riding in with me. Stay put here while I do what I get paid for.'

'You ain't thinking of riding in there alone against half a dozen of Bracknell's men, are you? They're all tough veterans from the war. You wouldn't stand a chance. Let me go with you and we'll give them a real fight.'

Loman shook his head. 'Stay back and I'll handle it,' he insisted.

He rode forward, reaching for his pistol and checking the weapon. He glanced over his shoulder once and saw Slattery sitting his horse where he had stopped. Then he faced his front and cantered into the big yard. A mounted guard, sitting his horse just in front of the ranch house and holding a rifle across his saddle horn, lifted the weapon when he failed to recognize Loman, who was waiting for a hostile move. His pistol hammered once and the bullet punched the guard out of his saddle.

Three men came running out of the bunkhouse, shooting as they emerged, and Loman triggered his smoking pistol, the heavy sounds of the shots ripping through the uneasy silence. He slid out of his saddle. When he looked for the trio he saw that two were down and the third was staggering back into the bunkhouse. Bracknell stood in the doorway of the house. He was holding a rifle in the crook of his right arm, the muzzle pointing at the ground. Loman gazed at him from a distance of twenty feet, his pistol covering the man.

'You've been riding roughshod around here for some time now, Bracknell,' he said easily. 'Lacey was in town earlier, and I killed him. It looks like your business, whatever it is, has been shot full of holes. So where is the gold? You must have some idea after the poking around you have done.'

'Who are you?' Bracknell countered. There was

impatience in his cold blue eyes. 'You're wearing a deputy sheriff badge but you're not a local lawman, are you?'

'I'm a Pinkerton detective with orders to take you in. Throw down the rifle and surrender.'

Bracknell made as if to lift the muzzle of his rifle and Loman spoke sharply.

'You'd never make it. I want you alive, Bracknell, but I'll kill you if I have to. Drop the rifle and put up your hands.'

'Don't be a fool!' Bracknell spoke sharply. 'You made a bad mistake leaving Slattery at your back. He's fixing to plug you.' He raised his voice and called loudly. 'Don't do it, Slattery. This man is a Pinkerton detective.'

Loman hurled himself to the ground and rolled. A gun blasted from behind and he heard a bullet strike the ground close to his fast-moving body. He looked for Bracknell. The major was lifting his rifle. Pausing for a split second, Loman sent a shot at Bracknell, and saw the man stagger and drop to one knee.

The next instant he was struck in the back by a blow like the kick of a mule. Pain darted through him like a flash of lightning and he was sent flying by the impact. He lost his hold on his gun and pitched forward on to his face in the thick dust of the yard, his senses failing as darkness engulfed him, swallowing him as completely as if he had fallen into a bottomless pit. . . .

Loman lay inert until lancing pain through his back jolted him to his senses. He lay for interminable moments while the process of returning consciousness filtered through him. At first his mind was blanked out by shock, but thoughts began to writhe in his brain and he clenched his teeth against throbbing agony as he forced himself to sit up.

His narrowed gaze fell upon the supine figure of Major Bracknell stretched out on the porch, rifle discarded, arms outstretched in the careless manner of a man who had crossed the Great Divide. Grunting at the pain stabbing through his body at each movement, Loman leaned on his left elbow and looked around for Slattery. He heard the sound of someone digging and narrowed his eyes.

A buckboard was in the corral, its team standing patiently with lowered heads. Loman recovered his pistol, which lay close by, and had to make several attempts to rise before eventually managing to stand upright. He checked his pistol and reloaded the cylinder with fresh shells from his cartridge belt. Hub Slattery's head was showing in a hole in the centre of the corral. Loman smiled despite his pain. It looked as though Slattery was preparing to run out, and planning to take the missing gold with him.

Loman went forward slowly, breathing shallowly, for each breath sent a pang of agony through his back. The bullet that had struck him from behind had angled outwards beneath the left shoulder-blade and lodged in his left arm. He held his pistol in his right hand, his gaze intent upon the toiling HS rancher, and reached the lip of the hole before his shadow fell upon the rancher and made Slattery aware of his presence.

Slattery froze, and then turned slowly to gaze up at

Loman with expressionless eyes.

'I thought I'd killed you,' he said through clenched teeth.

'You said you didn't get away with the gold,' Loman commented.

'I lied.' Slattery dropped the shovel and reached for the pistol tucked into his waistband. He was sweating profusely, his face contorted with the effort of digging. Sweat was running into his eyes and he blinked rapidly. He stayed his grab for the gun when he found himself looking into the steady muzzle of Loman's pistol and moved his hands out from his waist.

'You got more lives than a wagonload of cats,' he snarled.

'Get rid of the gun, and then carry on digging,' Loman ordered. 'I want to see the colour of that gold.'

Slattery paused for an interminable moment, as if considering his chances, and then shrugged as if resigning himself to the situation. He took hold of the butt of his pistol with forefinger and thumb and eased the weapon out of his waistband. He jerked his hand as if intending to throw the gun aside then flipped it up to make a last desperate play for success.

Loman triggered his Colt, aiming for Slattery's right shoulder. Slattery twisted and fell inertly into the bottom of the hole. Blood began to seep from his wound to stain the first of the gold ingots that had been uncovered.

Loman heard horses approaching and saw Kate riding in with Bill McKay. His gun suddenly seemed very heavy and he let it fall. He dropped to the ground, reviewing his instructions from Chicago, and realized that with the unearthing of the gold his case had ended. He sighed and lapsed into unconsciousness. When Kate got to him she was surprised to see a smile on his lips.